King

Jamie Begley

King

ISBN-13: 978-0692258323
ISBN-10: 0692258329

Prologue

"Are you sure you don't want me to stay?"

"No, Lily. Go home with your husband; Henry will stay. With all the medications they've given me, I'm just going to sleep anyway," King answered his daughter while his eyes surveyed the occupants of his hospital room.

His daughter, Lily, sat on the edge of his hospital bed, holding his hand. Her adopted sister, Beth, and her husband, Razer, both stood at the foot of his bed. The last occupant of the room was Lily's husband, Shade. He stood in the open doorway of the hospital room, his attention on the people in the room and those entering it.

King hadn't kept himself alive all these years in a variety of illegal activities without being a good judge of character. The man his daughter was married to was a scary son of a bitch, and he should know; he had seen a lot of scary shit with his own disreputable lifestyle. Fuck, he had stared down death since he was thirteen-years-old, and was an immoral son of a bitch, but Lily's husband had chills running down his back.

When Lily stood up, releasing his hand, King felt a brief moment of loss. It had been the first time she had ever voluntarily touched him. When he had kidnapped her from the church store where she worked, she had struggled against him, surprising him with how well she was able to defend herself. He had no doubt who had taught her those moves.

When he had found out whom his daughter had married, he had ordered a background check done by his bodyguard, Henry. However, the report Henry had brought back hadn't set off any of the alarms that were now shrilling their warning. In fact, he had been relieved she had married a man in the military, whose assets included a large amount of properties and a very healthy bank account. All the bare facts had been laid out before him.

Fuck. He should have known it was too good to be true; he must be slipping. Belonging to The Last Riders should have been a warning sign, but he had checked them out, also. Their survivalist company was very lucrative, and they'd had a few run-ins with the law, yet that was it. Hell, he certainly couldn't throw any stones because of that; his own police record spanned a decade before he'd become smart enough to cover his tracks.

All in all, he had been satisfied Lily would be cared for until he heard Digger had escaped. Trying to protect Lily, he had kidnapped her to keep her safe. Instead, he had almost gotten her killed. How was he to know The Last Riders had more connections than God? Lily had been safe where she was; he had been the one to fuck up. The accusation and anger on Shade's face made sure he knew it, too.

"I'll come back and check on you in the morning." Lily brushed a brief kiss on his cheek before moving away from his bed.

"All right."

Beth moved beside the bed as Lily moved away. "It's nice to learn that Lily and I both have a relative left."

"I was sorry to hear about your mother and father, Beth."

He saw the closed look that came over his cousin's

face. Beth's father, Seth Cornett, had been his uncle. He had never been a friendly bastard—the over-righteous asshole had always gotten on his nerves—but he had provided Lily a safe home, which was more than King had been able to do.

Razer and Shade both said brief goodbyes before following their wives out.

King was still staring at the doorway when Henry came inside the room, shutting the door.

King lay back against his bed, wincing at the pain in his chest, no longer trying to hide the pain he was in.

"You okay, Boss?"

"Tell the nurse she can give me something for the pain now."

As Henry pushed the call button, requesting the medication for him, King gritted his teeth against the pain. He had wanted to be clearheaded with Lily in the room, and as a result, it was now well past time for his meds.

The nurse came bustling into the room, giving him an injection then King waited for her to leave.

"What did you think?" he asked his friend.

Henry closed the door again after the nurse walked out.

"I think there's more to him than the bio I gave you." Henry frowned. He would blame himself if something showed up that he'd missed; however, he was going to have to deal with it.

King agreed with his assessment. He was willing to bet his fortune that Shade was hiding information from Lily. "I do, too. Do another check on him. This time don't go through our contacts on the force; use Jackal. If anyone can find out something, he will."

He had used the Predators several times over the years when he needed to be discreet. Henry took out his cell phone, making the call while King listened to the one-sided conversation.

"He's on it." Disconnecting the call, Henry moved to stand beside his bed. "What are you going to do if he comes back with bad news?"

His head turned on the stiff pillow. "Depends. I don't want to interfere because Lily loves him; it's obvious just from the way she looks at him. But, if it's as bad as I think it's going to be, then I'll have to step in."

"And do what?"

"Get rid of him. I didn't sacrifice raising my own daughter so she could have a better life just to see her get hurt again. She's had enough of that shit."

"It won't be easy. Did you see the one with him? You'll be taking on more than her husband."

"Call Jackal back. Include The Last Riders in his search. Tell him to find out anything and everything on them and their members." King closed his eyes as Henry moved away to follow his instructions, feeling the drugs the nurse had given him finally taking effect. He would be more clear-headed when he woke, but it would take a couple of days for Jackal to find out the information he wanted. It didn't matter, though; he would be stuck in the hospital at least that long.

When he was released, he would stay at the house he had leased since he had first brought Lily to Treepoint. He would get to know his daughter better, learn more about what kind of woman he and Brenda had created. For the first time in his life, he was going to be a father to Lily, whether she needed him or not. He had a lot to make up for, and if getting rid of a husband who didn't deserve her needed to happen, then he would do it. He wasn't going to let Lily down again.

Chapter One

Evie gripped Train's ass, pulling him closer. "Fuck me harder."

"Damn, Evie, you're fucking like you didn't just come ten minutes ago."

Her mouth went to his shoulder, biting down. Winding her legs around his waist, she raised her pussy to meet each of his hard thrusts.

"You must be doing something wrong then," she taunted the biker.

His thrusts grew harder, reaching the spot she needed him to reach. Her head rolled back and forth on the bed as she came, her hands releasing her grasp on his ass when he moved to her side.

Train's deep breathing brought a smile to her lips. "You must be getting old. You used to be able to go three rounds without getting winded."

"I'm not getting old; you're just getting hornier."

Evie's smile disappeared. She turned to the side so Train couldn't see her expression, shutting off her alarm clock before it went off. "I have to get ready for work."

"Cool, I'm off today so I'm going to catch up on my

sleep." He made no effort to get out of her bed, rolling over onto his stomach instead.

Evie went to her bathroom. She had inherited Razer's room since he had moved into the house he had built behind the clubhouse. Before, she usually just shared whoever's bed she had found herself in for the night; she actually preferred it that way. She was hardly ever in here unless there were two or more of them fucking. Jewell and Cash had left an hour ago, trying to catch a few hours of sleep before the day started.

Evie stepped into the shower, feeling the water waken her. She had gotten less than two hours' sleep the night before, and it was going to be a long day. After she had put her time in at the factory, she was going to have to catch a nap.

She soaped her body, rinsing away the smell of Train and the others she had shared her bed with the night before. Then, stepping out of the shower, she grabbed a towel, drying off before tackling the chore of untangling and brushing her long hair. She needed to get it cut, but there was just something about the men holding her hair while they fucked her that turned her on, so she kept it long. Pleasure always came before convenience.

She put on her dark blue t-shirt without bothering with a bra and then pulled on a tight pair of jeans. She looked at the time as she slid her watch on, hurrying into the other room for her shoes and jacket. It might have been only a short distance to the factory, but it was cold as fuck outside.

Going downstairs, she didn't take the time to get a cup of coffee; she would get one when she got to work. With barely a minute to spare, she walked into the factory, grateful she wouldn't receive a warning from Shade for being late again.

Going to her worktable she shared with Jewell, she plopped her ass down on a stool.

"Cutting it close, weren't you?"

"I lost track of time," Evie admitted to her friend.

"More like you decided to get a quickie before work."

Evie shrugged. "Train was in rare form, and I decided to take advantage of the opportunity."

Jewell laughed. "Ever since he fucked Killyama, it's like he's trying to prove his manhood."

"He sure as hell proved it to me last night." Evie grinned, getting up to get a cup of coffee. She was on the way back to her table when Shade came out of his office, motioning for her.

"What's up?" she questioned.

Shade opened his office door wider and Evie walked inside, taking a seat on the corner of his desk. He closed the door as he came back inside.

"I need you to do something for me."

"What do you need me to do?" Evie asked curiously, taking a sip of her hot coffee.

"Beth has been changing King's bandages, but she's tied up with Mrs. Langley and a new patient. She wanted to know if you would be able to stop by and take care of it for her."

"No problem. I'll stop by after lunch." There went her nap. "I thought he would head back to his home."

"He wants to stay and spend some time with Lily before he goes back."

"How's that working out for you?" She didn't try to hide her amused grin. Lily and Shade were both still in the honeymoon stage after getting married on Christmas Eve. It wouldn't be much fun sharing Lily with her father, especially since two of Lily's childhood friends were still visiting, also. Shade, who was a private person, had to feel like his life was being invaded.

As Shade sat down behind his desk, staring at her, Evie lost her amused expression, and was about to get up.

"He nearly got Lily killed. The stupid bastard couldn't protect her when she was a kid, but he thinks he can make up for it now." He leaned back in his chair, his deadly gaze pinning Evie in place. "He's supposed to go back to Queen City in a few weeks, though, so I can tolerate him that long. I'm planning on taking Lily to Alaska the first of the month anyway, and we're going to be gone for a few weeks so there won't be any need for him to stay."

"Lily will love it."

"I haven't told her yet."

"I won't say anything." And she wouldn't. Shade and she had shared many confidences over the years, many they had never confided with the rest of The Last Riders.

Shade nodded his head. "Penni has decided to go back to work for Kaden Cross. I'm not happy about it, but I can't change her mind. The only stipulation I was able to get out of her was that The Predators have to stay away from her."

Evie bet that hadn't been easy. Penni, Shade's half-sister, was just as headstrong as her brother, but other than that, they were as different as night and day. Shade's personality was dark and filled with swirling mysteries while Penni was sunny and bubbly.

"I want you to drive back with her and spend some time with her."

"To make sure she's safe?"

"Partially. Penni has always managed to watch out for herself, but I have another reason."

"Which is?"

"King. I want you to find out exactly what shit he's involved in and if it could touch Lily."

"And if it can?"

Shade remained quiet.

"All right. Let me know when she plans to head back, and I'll get packed. What reason did you give her for why I'm going back with her?"

"Brotherly concern."

Evie snorted. Shade loved his sister, but if he were really worried about her, he would call his mother and put an immediate stop to her going back.

"That works for me; I could use a vacation. Besides, Lily said her dad runs a strip club; I can always pick up a few new pointers."

"I doubt that. You could probably teach them a thing or two."

"I do try." Evie grinned, sashaying her ass to the door.

"Evie?"

She turned her head back to him. "Yeah?"

"Anything, one little piece of dirt that can get Lily hurt, and I want to know."

She lost her smile, seeing the grim resolution on his face. "Sure thing." She went out the door, hoping for Lily's sake she didn't find anything. It would be a shame for Lily to lose her father when she had just found him.

Chapter Two

Evie knocked on the door, smiling when it was opened by a large man in a suit.

"Hi, you must be Henry. I'm Evie. Beth sent me to take care of King today."

When the door opened wider, allowing her inside, Evie entered the nicely-furnished house. The dark-leather furniture gave the home a modern appearance without being over the top. She followed behind Henry as he walked down a short hallway, coming to a stop outside a door where he gave a brief knock, only opening it when he heard a response from the other side.

Evie's eyes swept across the large bedroom until her attention was caught by a man lying on the bed. He was wearing dark jeans and a white button-up shirt, and his rugged good looks were surprising to her. She had somehow expected Lily's father to be much older, not this aggressively-in-your-face, sexy male. Wow, Evie thought. The resemblance between Lily and her father was remarkable. Both had the dark hair, but it was the violet eyes that left no doubt about their relationship.

"Hello, I'm Evie."

"Beth called and said you would be taking her place today." The sound of his harsh voice had sparks running through her stomach. It suited his face.

Evie set her satchel containing her supplies on the chair beside his bed. "How are you feeling today?" Her nursing persona kicked in as she opened her bag and took out a clean pair of gloves.

"I'm doing well."

Evie turned back to him, seeing he was staring at her with an arched brow.

"Too much?" she questioned with a grin.

"A little."

Evie shrugged. "Old habits are hard to kill." She motioned for him to unbutton his shirt.

"You worked in a hospital?"

"Yes, when I was in the military and afterward. I was also a Corpsman in the field for nine months."

Evie watched as he unbuttoned his shirt, revealing a muscled and lean chest. He didn't even have the paunch she had assumed a man who made his living running a strip club would have. Somehow, she had imagined him short and stubby with a half-balding head. In reality, he was the direct opposite: muscular, with defined abs.

He flinched when she reached out to touch him. Startled, Evie's eyes lifted and were caught by his purple gaze. Surprisingly, she felt herself blush.

Her hands went to the bandage, carefully removing the tape before gently lifting the gauze away. It wasn't the worst gunshot wound she had ever seen. It didn't seem to be the worst injury he had dealt with during his lifetime, either. Her experience from being a Corpsman easily allowed her to identify the scars visible on his body.

A scar delivered from a knife was on his stomach. It was bad enough Evie assumed whoever had given it to him was doing his best to gut him. He had another scar on his side that showed he had been shot before, also. At the base of his throat, he had a thin scar she was barely able to see. Someone must have unsuccessfully tried to garrote him.

When his hands pulled his shirt back from his body, she saw the scars on both wrists that were signs he had been tied up and tortured. The cigarette burns on the back of his hands sickened her the most. Shade had told her how King had risen from poverty to fight and win control of Queen City. The brutality of that rise to power was exhibited on his body.

Silently, she disposed of the dirty bandages and her gloves before putting on a fresh pair and getting clean bandages.

Sitting down on the bed, she cleaned the wound that was beginning to heal then placed the clean bandage and taped it in place. Standing back up, she removed her gloves then disposed of them into the same trashcan.

She took out her thermometer, rolling it over his forehead; no fever. He was recovering well from being shot. Evie put her thermometer back in her bag, snapping it closed before lifting it and placing the strap back over her shoulder.

"That's it?" King asked.

"Yes, unless you're having any pain?"

"No."

"Then that's all Beth said needed to be done. Did she forget to tell me something?" Evie frowned, trying to remember if there was something she had forgotten in Beth's instructions.

"No." His brief, cranky reply had Evie cocking her head to the side and her inquisitive gaze searching his. "Beth usually brought me lunch when she came."

Evie's lip twitched. "She didn't tell me I should bring you lunch. Would you like me to go out and get you something?" Evie offered, wondering if he wanted something to eat, why he didn't get Henry to get it for him.

"No, Henry will take care of it."

"All right then. It was nice meeting you, Lily's father." She moved toward the door.

"Are you a friend of Lily's?"

"I like to think I am, yes."

"Her husband?"

"Yes."

"How close?"

Evie openly gaped at him. What was he trying to ask? "I have known Lily since she was a senior in high school, and I met Shade when we were in high school and served in the military together. So, I guess we're pretty good friends."

"I was just wondering since you stepped in for Beth today."

"Oh, I used to work with Beth a few years ago before the factory opened. I help out whenever she needs an extra hand."

"I see. It was nice meeting you."

Evie nodded her head, feeling as if he was dismissing her. She opened her mouth to say something then snapped it closed, remembering her friendship with Lily and Beth. She really didn't want to make them angry by calling Lily's father an arrogant asshole, but he was definitely riding the line of being just that with his attitude.

Evie went out the door, leaving it open, aware that Henry was following behind her. She walked to the front door, about to open it, but Henry reached out and opened it for her.

"He can be a little abrasive."

Evie heard the humorous edge to his voice; it probably wasn't the first time he had witnessed his boss pissing someone off. "No shit."

"He grows on you."

"I'll take your word for it." Evie went out the door and to her car, sliding in. She had begun looking forward to a vacation with Penni this morning after Shade had asked her to investigate King's businesses; now, she wasn't so sure. She had a feeling it wasn't going to be as simple as she had thought it would be. He sure as fuck didn't share his daughter's sweet personality.

* * *

"I think you made her angry."

King finished buttoning his shirt before giving Henry his attention. He lay back against the headboard of the bed. "I intended to. I wanted to see her reaction when I mentioned Shade."

He reached into his nightstand, pulling out a thick sheathe of papers then laying them across his lap as he continued reading the facts Jackal had been able to gather on The Last Riders. He wondered how much of it Beth and Lily were aware of.

"It's more of a sex club than a motorcycle club." King's hand tightened on one of the papers as he read.

Henry remained silent; his friend and bodyguard always knew when to keep his mouth shut, sensing his moods.

How could they become involved with such a group? He couldn't imagine Lily participating in the club's activities with her background, so he had to assume she was clueless.

"Lily and Beth both live in houses behind the club."

"Beth went back and forth between the club and her home before her house was built," King said. "Lily only moved into the clubhouse when the man Digger contracted to kill her botched up."

"Yes."

King continued reading. "Seems Evie is a little more than a nurse; she's a nurse practioner in the club, she was the first woman who became a member."

"So… she?"

"Participates in all the club's activities. She's over the women." King lifted another paper, his face turning grimmer as he read. "We were right about Shade."

"How bad?"

"He's an assassin for the military. He also contracts out

to other groups." A whistle left his lips. "He commands a pretty hefty fee to perform. How sure is Jackal about some of these hits?"

"Jackal doesn't make mistakes."

"I wish he had this time." King looked down at the paper in his hand. Lily's husband was a lethal bastard. His hits had a varied background and some he had heard of, some he hadn't. The ones he had were no loss; he would have killed them for free given the opportunity. It still made his gut clench that Lily was married to a man who could kill so effortlessly.

"Did you see his psych report? Jackal said he had to pay extra for that piece of information," Henry noted.

King picked up the report. "Make sure he's compensated."

"Already taken care of." Henry was efficient, managing to keep all his businesses under his watchful eyes.

King read Shade's psych report. When he finished, he knew there was no way he could allow the man to remain married to Lily. He read through the remaining papers, finding out all the relevant information he needed to know about the remaining members.

"They're a deadly group of men; each has his own particular skill."

"It won't be easy taking them on."

"When have I ever been afraid of a challenge?" King eyed Henry.

"She won't thank you for it. She's in love with him."

"There's no way Shade's in love with her. I'd be surprised if he even bled. The psychiatrist who did that psych doesn't even think he's fucking human."

"According to women, he's human." King stared at his friend coldly, letting him know he didn't appreciate his humor.

"He has to be hiding that from Lily. There is no way she would let him dominate her; she was too traumatized as a child."

This time, Henry remained wisely silent.

King sighed, throwing the papers to his side.

"What are you going to do?"

"What in the fuck do you think I'm going to do?"

Chapter Three

Evie went back to the clubhouse. Once inside, she decided not to take her nap; instead she pitched in to help Bliss and Raci cook dinner.

"So, what was he like?" Bliss asked.

Evie didn't have to ask whom she was referring to. "He's younger than I thought he would be, and kind of sexy." Both women stared at her. Evie grinned, raising her hands in the air. "Well, he is."

"I've got to see this guy," Jewell said.

"Who?" Beth asked, coming into the kitchen.

The women went silent.

Evie decided she might as well tell. "I was just telling them that King was younger than I thought and not bad looking, either."

"Yes, he is attractive." Beth didn't seem to be disturbed by everyone talking about her cousin. "How did it go at his house today?"

"Pretty well, considering I think he was fishing for information on Shade."

"I thought he might. He asked me a few questions about Shade, too. I think that's pretty understandable."

"Why? It's not like he raised her," Raci butted in.

"No, but he did keep an eye out for her." Evie could see Beth was going to defend her cousin, so she changed the subject to getting dinner done. One by one, the men came in from the factory, filling their plates. Evie fixed her own plate and then took a seat at the table. She was tired and didn't really pay much attention to the conversation going on around her, so when she was finished, she got up from the table.

"Evie, I forgot to ask, would you mind taking care of King again tomorrow? This one patient I have has me behind on all my others, and Ton has the flu. I wanted to stop by his house and check on him tomorrow."

"Sure, I don't mind. Should I take him lunch? He didn't seem happy that I came without it today."

Beth blushed. "I've been fixing him a plate at lunch and taking it. If it's not too big a hassle, would you mind?"

"That's fine. I think it put him in a bad mood."

"That's his normal personality."

"Then I'd hate to actually see him in a bad mood."

"Hell, Evie, what man can stay in a bad mood with you around?" Train came up behind her, putting his hand on her ass.

"Plenty," Evie said, moving away from his touch; she was too tired to mess around tonight.

She stacked her dirty dishes then went upstairs to her room, getting ready for bed. She turned out her light then locked the door. It had been a while since she had locked the men out, but she needed a good night's sleep. She was getting older; the all-nighters were becoming fewer and fewer.

She didn't know if it was because she was getting bored, but she had told Shade the truth—she was looking forward to a vacation. Working at the factory all day and partying all night was becoming old. She had begun thinking lately of going back to work with Beth or the hospital. The time in Queen City would give her time to make her mind up.

Evie rolled over onto her stomach, thinking about Lily and the expression on King's face. She had a feeling King wasn't happy with Lily's marriage. She hoped the man kept his thoughts to himself; Shade wouldn't be happy with his interference.

Evie shivered under the covers. She hated the thought of the two men not getting along. King and Shade both were used to getting their own way, and while King might be used to dealing with the seedier side of life, she was sure he had never dealt with someone of Shade's caliber. If he took Shade on, it was a battle he wouldn't win, and he would very likely end up out of Lily's life forever.

* * *

The next day, Henry opened the door before she could knock. She flashed him a smile as she stepped into the house, handing him the plate of food Beth had made for him.

"You'll need to reheat that before giving it to him."

"Okay." He walked her down the hallway, knocking on the door before opening it for her and closing it behind her.

As she entered, she saw King was sitting at a chair by the window.

"Hello. How are you doing today?" Evie asked brightly, her chirpy voice making her wince at herself.

"Fine." His mocking gaze had her smile disappearing. "Do you want me to move to the bed?"

"No. I can do it where you are." Evie set her satchel on the desk, opening it to put her gloves on. When she turned around, King hadn't unbuttoned his shirt. "You can unbutton your shirt."

He unbuttoned his shirt, keeping his eyes on her the whole time. Evie waited patiently, not letting him embarrass her. When he finished, she jerked the tape off.

"Ouch."

"Sorry." That would teach the bastard. She didn't know

what he was up to, but she wasn't a young girl or dependent on him for a payday; she didn't have to tolerate his behavior.

She threw away her dirty gloves and the bandages, going to her satchel for fresh ones. She then cleaned his wound and placed a fresh bandage on. When she finished, she took his temperature.

"You're healing well. No temperature." Evie closed her satchel.

Henry came in the door then, carrying the food. Placing it down on the desk, he brought a small table to place in front of King then set the food down in front of him.

"Thanks for bringing me lunch," King said to Evie before he began eating.

Evie shrugged. "It was no big deal; we always have plenty. The men all have big appetites." Evie winced at her poor choice of words.

Evie stood still, waiting silently for him to make an ugly comment.

"Anything wrong?"

"Does he always wait on you like that?"

"Henry?" His violet eyes stared back at her cynically.

"Yes. You got a problem getting off your ass and doing stuff for yourself?"

"No, I went for a walk and tired myself out. Henry had to help me back to the bedroom."

Fuck. She should have kept her mouth closed; it was no business of hers whether Henry wiped King's ass for him.

"Sorry, I should have minded my own business. You should have told me you weren't feeling well. I would have checked you over better." She set her satchel back down, starting to open it.

"I'm fine. I just overdid it."

"You're sure?"

"Yes." His lips twitched.

Evie closed her satchel again. "You only need to be walking around your house. It's too soon to be doing much more than that."

"I'll keep that in mind." Evie nodded her head, picking up her satchel again.

"Lily, Beth, and their husbands are coming for dinner Friday. Would you like to come?" *Hell, no*, Evie thought, about to turn down the invitation. "I thought it would make Razer and Shade more comfortable to have another acquaintance here."

Evie thought quickly. If King said something to piss off Shade, it might be better to have someone else here to help pull him off King. Not that she would be much help, but at least he wouldn't punch her like he would Razer for interfering.

"Yes, thank you. I'd like that."

"Good. I thought it could give everyone something to do on a Friday night. It's not like this town has a lot to keep you busy. What does everyone do to keep themselves occupied?"

Evie swallowed. Somehow, he knew. Like a snake about to strike, he was waiting for her reaction. Evie's face went impassive. "We go to the movies."

"I'm glad to provide a better option this week."

"I'll see you Friday then. Make sure you tell Beth if you're not feeling better tomorrow." Evie turned, leaving the room before he could say anything else. She almost ran into Henry as she got to the front door. The man was determined to beat her to the fucking door.

"Later, Henry."

"Goodbye, Evie."

Evie released the breath she had been holding. Going to her car, she threw her satchel into the backseat, pulling out her cell phone before she put her key in the ignition. Finding Shade's number, she hit dial.

"We need to talk."

* * *

21

King looked up from his plate when the door opened again. "Well?"

"The phone was in her hand before she backed out of the driveway.

"Good."

"King...?"

"What?"

"Be careful. This guy doesn't mess around. The two responsible for Lily getting hurt were found at the bottom of a mountain not far from here. They crashed their bikes and went headfirst over the guardrail. It took a helicopter to get their bodies out."

"He doesn't fuck around, does he?" It wasn't a question; it was a statement.

"No, he doesn't."

"I'll be careful. I don't plan on being stupid."

"Making him aware you know what's going on at the club might not be smart."

"It's merely gossip I could have found at the local diner. Besides, I know exactly how I'm going to bring Shade down."

"How?"

"Evie. I'll find out everything I need to bring down the club from her."

"You think you can get her to betray her club?"

King didn't say anything, giving his friend a confident smile.

"She might be able to resist your charms."

"When has any woman turned me down? Plus, she's a whore. She fucks all the men in The Last Riders and most of the women. Why would she turn me down?"

Henry didn't say anything, taking the dirty dishes and moving the small table back against the wall.

"Henry?"

"I don't think she's going to be as easy to fool into ratting out her friends. All those reports you've been reading show how loyal they are to each other, so I don't see her breaking so easily."

"Did I say it was going to be easy? I think she'll fight her attraction to me, but she'll cave and tell me everything I need to know once I have her in my bed. I don't know which I'm going to enjoy more: fucking her or getting Shade out of Lily's life."

Chapter Four

"That was all he said?" Shade's enigmatic gaze rested on her, waiting for her response.

"Yes, I think he knows about the club."

"Perhaps. It wouldn't be difficult with Kaley telling everyone in town."

"You think that's all?"

"No, I think he's checked us out. I'm sure he has the resources to find out what he wants."

"It doesn't bother you?"

"No, Lily knows the truth about the club. He's not going to tell her anything I haven't."

"You've told her everything?" Evie was shocked, her heart beating rapidly at his statement.

"Not everything, no. Just the parts King can use against me. The rest about my jobs with the military, no."

"Did you tell her about me?" Evie licked her dry lips.

"No."

"Thank you. So, what are you going to do?"

"Nothing. I'm going to let him make his move."

"You don't think he can come between you and Lily?" she asked hesitantly.

"No. I'm really not worried about some bullshit he thinks he's going to pull out of the closet. If he does, Lily and I will deal with it."

"Cool. I could just picture you beating the shit out of him with Lily watching. That's why I accepted his dinner invitation."

"When I deal with King, Lily won't be around. I can deal with him, man to man, whatever he pulls. It's the garbage that could get Lily killed that concerns me."

"When is Penni going back to Queen City?"

"The week after next. The same week Lily and I leave for Alaska. I told her last night."

"Is she excited?"

"That's putting it mildly." A smile lit his face briefly. It never failed to stun Evie when she saw that look on his face. Shade had loved Lily since he had seen her as a senior in high school; however, he had waited until she had finished college before marrying her.

"You finished for the day?"

"Yeah, I just have to lock up." When they walked out of the office, Evie stood by his side as he locked the factory door before going up to the clubhouse together. Dinner was already starting when she turned to go upstairs. Shade paused.

"You're not going to eat?"

"No, I'm not hungry. I'm going to have an early night. See you in the morning."

"Night."

Evie went upstairs to her room, taking a shower before she lay down on her bed to watch television. She heard Raci and Jewell in the bedroom next door with Cash. A knock came at her door, which she ignored before whomever it was went away.

Sitting up in bed, she ran her hands through her hair. She didn't know what was wrong with her lately. She hopped off the bed, going to the mini-fridge and taking out a beer before climbing back on the bed.

It was late before she turned off her TV to go to sleep. Her body was restless, but she wasn't in the mood to fuck. As a picture of the man she really wanted flashed through her mind, Evie flung her arm over her eyes, trying to shut out his image. It wouldn't do any good, though; it never did.

* * *

The next day, Evie was the first one at the factory. She had already started filling an order when the other workers began coming in. Jewell and Raci came in the door together, coming to a stop when they saw her already at work.

"What got you out of bed so early?" Jewell asked as she took the workstation next to hers.

"Went to bed early. Besides, I saw the orders were beginning to back up with Lily working fulltime at the church store and Georgia in jail." Shade had given Georgia's brother a job to replace Georgia, but he'd had to start at the entry-level position, not floor supervisor like his sister. They had also hired another worker to fill Lily's spot, but he was still training; it took time to learn where everything was in the factory.

They could actually hire more workers, but they wanted to be careful with the ones they hired, preferring to give fewer workers better pay and keeping the company stable. Orders could dry up, and they didn't want to lay off workers who were already well acquainted with layoffs.

"Can I get you something, Evie?"

She glanced up from taping her package closed. "No. Thanks, Charlie." He was overly anxious to please. Charlie had been hired when Lily had asked Shade. With two kids and a sweet wife, their situation had tugged at Lily's heart. It had been hard to find another job in construction when he had hurt his back and was unable to do the strenuous work.

"Jewell?"

"I got it covered." He turned away, pulling his own

order.

"He's a nice guy."

"Yeah, I can see how Lily wanted to help. Have you met his wife and kids? Breaks your heart. They've had it so hard. Viper and Razer loaded up the truck and took them groceries. When they came back, they told Shade to take his pay up. It must have been bad."

Evie swallowed hard. Until she had come to Treepoint, she hadn't really understood the extreme poverty of the area. At first, she couldn't understand why they didn't move away to a better area with more opportunities. Many of the younger population did, but many stayed. After living there for a while, she realized the rich heritage of the town; the mountains and close family bonds were what held them in place.

Shade came in, going to his office, and the work increased to a busy vibe. Up until summer, the factory had been run in a rotating month by each of The Last Riders, taking turns. After his last rotation, Shade had stayed longer, his skill at running the factory apparent by the increase of orders.

As the day flew by, Evie hadn't felt so good in a long time, reinforcing her belief that she had been partying too hard the last year. It was time to calm down and take a breather, at least from the alcohol and weed she had been junking up her body with.

"Finished?" Jewell broke the silence.

"Yes." Evie tossed her last order into the mail cart before going out the steel door.

The bright sunlight in the parking lot had her and Jewell hesitating. When her eyes were able to focus, a big smile lit her face at what she was seeing.

"Hot damn." Jewell took the words right out of her mouth.

Running forward, she threw herself into the arms of the man unpacking his belongings from the trunk of his car.

"Lucky, welcome home." When a grin lit his face, Evie thought it was the first authentic one she had seen in years. He had taken on being an undercover agent by posing as Pastor Dean at the local church. After Christmas, it had finally come to a head, and he was able to close an investigation that had been ongoing for years.

"Why didn't you tell us you were moving in today?" Evie asked.

"Because I didn't know. The new pastor arrived in town last night. Do you remember Merrick Patterson? He was looking for a new church. His wife is expecting and the extreme cold weather up north was getting to her, so he jumped at the chance to move."

"Merrick?" Evie remembered him from the military. He and Lucky both had been chaplains.

"That's fantastic." Evie went to church every Sunday. She had been dreading the possibilities of who would be taking over the church; a sanctimonious preacher would have made it difficult to attend. "Let me help you with your bags."

"Razer and Viper just took one load for me, and there's not much more. I threw all my suits away. I don't want to see another suit for the rest of my life."

Evie quit smiling. Lucky was one of the best pastors she had ever known. He had a natural ability to draw people out. He, on the other hand, felt he had lost the calling.

After Evie heard the factory door open and close, Shade came to stand beside them. "I see you're not wasting any time."

"No. I wanted to make Merrick comfortable. I'll hand over the church to him Sunday, and then I'll be free of all my commitments to the church."

"We need to talk," Shade said just as Lily pulled into the parking lot.

"Fuck," Lucky said. Lily was a member of Lucky's church and was one of his most faithful followers. It was going to be hard for her to see the other side of Lucky that she was unfamiliar with.

"Be cool," Shade warned Lucky.

"Pastor Dean, hi. I was wondering where you were today," Lily said as she came up to the group.

"I'm outta here," Jewell said under her breath.

"Coward," Evie teased.

"I'm a lover, not a fighter. Arguments tense me up." Jewell left, but Evie wasn't about to budge from the spot. She was dying to know how the men were going to work this out.

"Hi, Lily. I was going to come back and introduce you to the new pastor because you were at lunch with King when I came by the church store earlier."

"You went to lunch with King?" Shade asked sharply.

"At the diner," Lily answered.

"Why didn't you tell me?"

"I wasn't aware I had to tell you my every move since the danger is over."

"We'll talk about this later."

"No, we won't. It was lunch, just across the street."

"Lily, we still don't know who Digger hired to hurt you. Until we make sure he's stopped, you're not completely out of danger."

"Oh." She paused. "Next time, I'll tell you when I leave the church."

Round One went to Shade, but at least Lily hadn't caved in to his demand without question.

Lily turned back to Lucky expectantly. "Are you staying for dinner?"

"Actually, dinner and breakfast. I'm moving in."

"That's great. I was worried you would move away, and I wouldn't see you anymore."

"I think you're going to be seeing a lot more of Lucky than you ever expected to see." Evie couldn't help herself. Shade and Lucky's hard stare didn't faze her, either. She was looking forward to seeing how they were going to handle Lily.

"Let's go home, Lily," Shade said, taking Lily's arm and moving her toward the pathway to their new home he had built behind the clubhouse.

"Spoil sport." Evie called after them.

"You're feeling brave today." Lucky slid a box out of the truck, handing it to her then took another for himself.

"Not necessarily. Lily was here. You can get away with all kinds of shit when she's around."

"I see you're taking advantage of the situation."

"Fuck, yes. Of course, he pays us back later, but it's worth it."

"I'll take your word for it. He might give you an extra shift or dock your pay; however, he'll just beat the shit out of me when she leaves."

"Don't be a pussy."

"I'll try."

They carried the boxes up the steps to the clubhouse as Viper and Razer were both coming down.

"We put you in Knox's old room. That cool?"

"That's perfect. He had the biggest bed," Lucky said, going up the steps.

Razer took the box from Evie, following him up the steps.

"I take it he's going to make up for lost time?" Viper said.

"I bet he hasn't even had a blowjob in the last five years. What do you think?" Evie asked flippantly.

Viper laughed. "I better warn the women."

"Too late." Jewell's seductive voice could be heard coming from the upstairs.

Evie went into the kitchen where Bliss and Stori were finishing cooking dinner and most of the members were already in line. Evie took a plate.

"Lucky is upstairs," she said casually. When Bliss, Stori and Ember put their plates down, leaving the room at once, Evie got in the shortened line. Winter shook her head at her.

"You're not joining them?" Train asked, surprised.

"No. I'm going to let them have Lucky while I reap the benefits of the rest of the men." Evie began filling her plate.

"Just save some for me."

Evie knew he wasn't talking about the food. "Don't I always?"

Chapter Five

It took several attempts before she managed to shove a snoring Train off her. Sliding out from between him and Cash, she managed to get out of the bed. Evie stretched languidly, staring at the two male bodies sprawled on the bed, tempted to climb back in. Regretfully, she went to the bedroom door, going to her own room to get ready for work.

Dressing in a sweatshirt and jeans, she drew on her fur-lined boots. She would be glad when the last of winter was done. She hated cold weather, and Kentucky winters seemed to drag on forever.

Once she got to work, the factory was busy, so there wasn't much time to talk. It was almost the end of the day before Evie remembered tonight was the night she was supposed to have dinner at King's house.

After work, she went to her room. Looking through her closet, she studied her clothes, trying to decide what to wear. Evie was certain Lily and Beth would both wear dresses, yet she hated wearing dresses and dressing up. However, she did have several church dresses she could pick from.

Pulling out a black dress shorter than her church dresses, she showered before changing into it. The deep V showed a small amount of her breasts, but it wasn't over the top. Evie brushed her hair, pinning it on top of her head, and then stepped back to stare at her reflection.

Her hand grasped the dresser. It had been several years since she had seen the reflection staring back at her, and the elegant woman she glimpsed had not been missed. The painful memories her image brought had Evie taking down her hair, brushing it out and leaving it loose.

Going back to her closet, she took out a dark navy dress that wasn't as formal and was fitted on her body. Shade had texted her that he and Lily were ready to leave, so she slid on a pair of heels and headed downstairs, meeting them by the front door.

"You look pretty tonight, Evie," Lily complimented her.

"Thanks, Lily. You look gorgeous." She was wearing a dark purple dress that highlighted her violet eyes.

"You ready?" Shade asked.

Evie got her coat out of the closet and put it on. "Ready."

It took twenty minutes to get to King's house from the clubhouse. Evie sat near the passenger door while Shade drove Cash's old truck with Lily sitting in the middle. As he pulled into the driveway, Evie hoped the night wasn't going to be a disaster.

When Henry opened the door for them, King was sitting in the living room. Evie watched silently as Lily greeted her father, bending down to hug him and brushing a soft kiss on his cheek.

"Shade."

"King."

Evie saw the two men size each other up. Shade had dressed in his good jeans, boots and a nice black shirt. King's eyes flicked over Shade's relaxed attire. Shit. Evie could see where the night was headed within three minutes of walking into the door.

"Evie," King greeted her.

She gritted her teeth against his condescending tone. The man was fucking unbelievable. "King." She allowed her voice to be as condescending as the queen of fucking Sheba.

A twist of his lips showed she had made her point.

"Henry, get everyone a drink."

Lily's wary look as she sat down on the leather couch showed how little King knew his daughter. She was still uncomfortable being around liquor. While she was around it more constantly at the clubhouse, she didn't think the woman would ever lose the fear it inspired; her scars ran too deep.

Neither Lily nor Shade had ever explained Lily's reasons for her fears, but if it was as bad as the shadows that used to be in her eyes, Evie didn't want to know. She had heard enough on the night the basement had caught on fire to break her heart, and Evie hadn't thought that was possible. She had seen too many tragedies during her lifetime to be squeamish; however, what she had found out that night had been horrendous.

Evie was sitting down on a chair when the doorbell rang again. As Beth and Razer came into the living room, Beth was much more casual with King, giving him a hug and inquiring how he felt.

"I'm almost back to normal."

Normal wouldn't be how she characterized the granite-faced man who sat with his glass of bourbon in his hand.

"Dinner's ready." Henry's voice broke the silence in the room.

Evie gratefully got to her feet, going into the dining room. The table had been set lavishly. Both Shade and King sat on opposite ends of the table, so Evie took an open seat, unfortunately, the one next to King.

She took a tiny sip of her wine before picking up her water glass. The food was delicious—a standing rib roast with fingerling potatoes and asparagus tips—making Evie want seconds. She was glad she had restrained herself, though, when Henry brought out a chocolate mousse that was decadent.

She licked the small amount from her lips, feeling King's eyes on the movement. His eyes caught hers before Evie tore her gaze away, looking down at her empty bowl.

"Would you like more?"

"No, I think that was enough." She let her voice carry her warning. She wasn't going to play along with his attempted flirtation.

He nodded his head, turning his attention to Lily. "Would you like more?"

"Yes, please. I have a weakness for chocolate."

Evie finished her water while dessert was eaten, and when they went back into the living room, Evie had started to relax. The dinner had gone well and the night was almost over.

"How do you like working in the church store, Lily?"

"I love it. The Christmas holidays have left our shelves almost bare, though. So, we're having a clothing and food drive this Sunday after church. There's supposed to be a break in the weather. Pastor Dean—I mean, Lucky—thought it would be a good way for the new pastor to meet the congregation."

"I'll have to attend. It will be a good time to meet the rest of your friends."

"That would be nice."

"You're content at the store instead of using your degree? After all, anyone can be a cashier."

Here we go, Evie thought, seeing the others in the room stiffen at the indirect insult.

"No, I really like it. It's more than being a cashier. I have to approve of the needs of the people coming in—"

"I'm glad you don't feel like you're settling with the job opportunities available in Treepoint." King's interruption of Lily talking didn't sit well with Shade or Beth. Razer wasn't much happier, but he was able to hide it better.

"Lily's excellent at her job. Several families in the community have benefited from Lily working there. She's also helping them find jobs." Shade's arm went around Lily's shoulder, and her eyes smiled up into his.

Evie swallowed the lump in her throat. The woman was deeply in love with Shade, and anyone staring at Shade could see he returned her feelings. King, on the other hand, seemed unmoved by the touching sight of the newlyweds.

"So, how did you two meet?"

"We met at the lake when I was in high school."

Lily's choice of words had King straightening in his chair, his indolent attitude disappearing. "You allowed her to date a man of his age while she was still in school?" His accusation was directed at Beth, who paled at his harsh words.

"Of course not! I started dating Razer when Lily was in high school. As they were friends, naturally she met Shade. However, Lily and Shade didn't start seeing each other until last summer."

"A whirlwind courtship?"

"We had known each other for years." Shade's voice equaled King's in attitude.

Lily's head went back and forth between the men until her eyes settled on King. "I didn't feel rushed, if that's what you're getting at." Lily took Shade's hand in hers, gripping it tightly.

"I didn't mean to insinuate it was. I'm sorry if I implied otherwise."

Bullshit, Evie thought.

"I'm very happy, King. Shade and I are looking forward to a long and happy marriage with children."

"You're not pregnant, are you? You've only been married a month."

Shit, here we go. Lily's crestfallen expression had Shade's hand on her jaw, raising her face to his. He leaned over and placed a kiss on her lips that even had Evie blushing. Lily's face was bright red when Shade let her lips go.

"Lily and I are both anxious to start our family, but no, she isn't pregnant. Yet."

King opened his mouth to reply.

"I think that's wonderful, Lily. You're going to make a great mother," Evie said, cutting in before King had the chance.

King's mouth snapped closed at her words, and she saw his hands clench on the arms of the armchair he was sitting on.

Beth rose to her feet. "Tomorrow may be Saturday, but I have to be at work early. Lily, you and Evie have to be at the church early, too, remember? The luncheon we're having for Pastor Patterson and his wife?"

"Yes. Rachel is helping, too, and Willa is bringing dessert. You're right; we should go. I don't want to tire you, King." When Lily got to her feet, thanking Beth silently for stepping in, Evie rose to her feet, also.

Lily went to King, reaching up to brush his cheek with a kiss. "I hope to see you Sunday."

When Lily would have turned away, King took her hand. "You haven't called me Dad since I was shot."

Evie could tell from the expression on Lily's face that the woman didn't know how to respond. Evie took a step forward, reaching her hand out for King to take. He released Lily reluctantly to take her hand.

"Thanks for dinner, King." Evie maneuvered her body, giving Lily the opportunity to slip away. King tracked her movements before coming back to hers.

"Will I be seeing you Sunday, too?"

"I'll be at the church," Evie confirmed. She would be there, but she didn't know why it mattered to him.

"Good, I'll look forward to it."

Evie nodded, unable to bring herself to say the same.

She took a deep breath of fresh air when she was finally

outside. It could have gone worse. It didn't take a genius to figure out King wasn't happy with Lily's choice of husband, but Lily and Shade were leaving Monday for Alaska and King would be headed back to Queen City.

Evie walked to the truck, sliding in next to Lily. It was quiet on the way back to the clubhouse.

The sooner he left, the better. What damage could he do from Queen City?

Chapter Six

Evie placed the large cake on the center of the dessert table where they had set up the recreation room.

"Willa, the cake is too pretty to cut." Evie turned back to the woman who had brought the cake.

Her friendly face flushed from the compliment. "Thank you for helping me carry it in, Evie."

"I didn't mind. I managed to swipe a taste or two along the way." Evie smiled, licking the tip of her finger.

"That just makes a man want to miss lunch and go straight for dessert."

Evie braced herself before replying to King. He had managed to come up to them when she wasn't paying attention. Damn cake. Her sweet tooth had managed to get her in trouble more than once.

As soon as Willa noticed a man was near, she closed down her smile, becoming more contained.

"Willa, this is King, Lily's father," Evie performed the introductions. *If the asshole says one thing out of place to her, I will smack him upside his head*, she promised herself.

Willa was extremely shy and self-conscious of her weight. Personally, Evie didn't think it was anyone else's business but her own, yet the woman had received many ugly comments from people who were insensitive and uncaring about hurting her.

"It's nice to meet you," Willa murmured.

"Did you bake the cake?"

Willa nodded.

"I've been to several large cities and a variety of states, and that cake is one of the most beautiful ones I've seen."

"Thank you."

"Do you own a shop?"

"No, I bake at home. It keeps me busy enough."

"Well, if you decide to open a store, let me know. I would invest not only my money, but my stomach, to opening one."

Even Evie had to laugh at his expression staring at the cake.

"I'll keep that in mind." Willa lost her self-consciousness, asking King where he was from.

"Did you bring a cake?" Lucky's voice filled with disbelief, interrupting King's description.

"Yes." Willa's startled eyes flew to Lucky's.

"You baked a cake to greet the new minister, but never made me one?" Lucky's accusing eyes were on Willa's embarrassed face. Evie wanted to kick the dumb man.

"I wouldn't have baked you one, either. Do you remember when you took over? There were three tables of food and four for desserts."

"There was?"

"Yes, there was," Evie confirmed.

"I actually made you a cake when you arrived." Willa's soft voice was filled with embarrassment.

"Georgia packed it in. When you saw her, you assumed she had made it."

Lucky was the one turning red now. "I'm sorry. I didn't know."

"It doesn't matter; you ate it. I brought it for you to eat, not for the compliments." All the single women in the parish had filled the tables, trying to get his attention, but Willa had let someone else take credit for her cake. "Excuse me. I haven't met the new pastor yet." Willa moved away toward the new minister, whose wife was standing by his side.

Pastor Patterson was handsome and the same age as Lucky. If he hadn't been married, the women would have been all over him. From his wife's glare, Evie sensed she wasn't going to tolerate any women becoming too friendly with her husband.

Brooke Patterson's rounded belly showed she was pregnant, although Evie couldn't imagine her being a mother. The cold bitch hid her true colors from Merrick, but Evie was fully aware of who she really was.

When she had walked into the church and saw Brooke, she had been stunned, almost leaving. The only reason she had stayed was because Evie knew the manipulating woman would find a way to use it to her advantage.

Brooke's eyes swept Willa from head to toe. After Willa introduced herself she held her hand out to Pastor Patterson, who took it, greeting her back. When he released it, he then introduced her to his wife.

"Dean told me you teach bible study for the youth on Wednesday. I'll be taking it over if you don't mind. I consider it my duty as the Pastor's wife. I hope you don't mind?"

"No."

It wouldn't matter if she did, Evie thought, since Brooke hadn't really given Willa the choice.

"Anything I can do to help you settle in to your new church—" Willa began.

"We have an abundance of volunteers. Of course, they're all women," Brooke broke in snidely.

True to form, her frostbitten greeting to Willa proved too much for her to handle, and soon after, Evie saw Willa leaving. King and Lucky noticed, also.

"Where's she going?" Lucky asked.

"She's leaving," Evie said sadly. She would be surprised if Willa came back.

"Why?" Lucky asked. "She's not even going to give him a chance?"

"She did."

Lucky was dressed in slacks and a shirt. He was dressed nicely but had not worn a suit, sticking to his promise of not donning one again. Men like Lucky would never understand a woman like Willa, but Merrick's wife had; that was why she had managed to frighten Willa off.

"Let's eat. I'm hungry." Evie moved toward the table. She had directed her comment to Lucky, but King was the one who stood next to her, fixing a plate for himself.

Evie couldn't resist. "You didn't bring Henry to fix your plate?"

"He's here, but he's too worried about stuffing his own face to worry about me." King nodded to Henry sitting at one of the tables with two plates in front of him.

"Every man for himself?"

"When someone else is cooking, yes."

As Evie laughed, sitting down at a table, King sat down next to her. "Where's Lily?"

"She's downstairs at the church store with Rachel. Several parishioners brought their donations in today. She'll be up later."

When King took a bite of a casserole, his expression had Evie handing him several napkins. She continued eating her own food while he tried to rinse out his mouth with his iced tea.

"Gina made that. Never been to a hometown potluck?"

"No." His strangled voice had Evie giving him advice.

"Next time, take a small bite until you're sure if you like it or not. Of course, I do have the hometown advantage and know the best cooks."

"You knew it was going to taste bad?" King asked, taking another drink of tea.

"I was hoping she was improving. At Christmas, she

made a potato casserole that was almost edible. That looked really good; I was waiting to see if it was before I got some. I guess I won't be making a trip back."

King's next bite was tiny as he chewed thoughtfully. "You could have given me a warning."

"I figured you deserved it after last night."

"What did I do last night?"

Evie set her fork down. "I haven't known you long, but I don't think you seem to be stupid. Unless I'm mistaken."

"No." King's friendliness disappeared into the wind.

"Then don't act like you don't know what the fuck I'm talking about."

"You're cussing in church?"

"I'm pretty sure God knows you're an ass."

King burst into laughter. "You're right. It's not like I can hide it."

"You make no effort to hide your dislike of Shade, and if you don't cut it out, you're going to lose Lily as quickly as you decided to finally be a father."

King's face turned to granite. "It's none of your business."

"Then don't make snide comments to my friends in front of me. I might not know a lot about you, King, but I'm telling you that Shade loves Lily. He'll make her a good husband."

"Does Lily know you've fucked her husband?"

Evie almost picked her plate up and threw it at him. Instead, she didn't show any reaction other than to start rising to her feet.

King grabbed her arm. "Sit down."

"Take your hand off me now. There's something you need to know. I'm not intimidated by you, and unlike Lily, I don't give a damn about you. I was trying to help because I sincerely see you want a relationship with Lily, but I can see now she's better off not being around you."

King's hand dropped to his side. "I'm sorry. I'm too sensitive about Lily and I overreacted. Please, finish eating.

I'll keep quiet."

"I've lost my appetite." When she got to her feet again, he let her go.

Evie put her plate in the trashcan then left without saying goodbye to Merrick and his wife. She should have escaped when Willa had and saved herself a headache.

"You're leaving already?" King said from behind her.

She just couldn't catch a break.

"Yes, I'm going home," Evie said quickening her step back to her car as King effortlessly kept up.

"Anxious to get back home to all the men?" he said cynically.

Evie came to an abrupt stop. "If you've got something to say, spit it out."

"All right, I will." His casual stance with his hands in his pant pockets was calm and collected while Evie's temper was soaring.

"You fuck them all or just certain ones? Do Beth and Lily participate in the orgies?"

Evie's hand flew up to smack him in the face, but he grabbed her wrist before she could hit him.

"You fucking bastard." Evie tried to jerk away from him. "It's none of your business what goes on at the clubhouse. You're the one who almost got Lily killed. You were the one who was responsible for a killer to put a hit out on her, but you kidnapped her anyway, taking her away from where she was safe and nearly getting her shot. Do women always take the hit for you?"

King's hand dropped away, his face paling. "I made a mistake. I thought I was keeping her safe. How was I supposed to know the whole town was Fort Knox?"

"If you had taken the time to get to know Lily, then you wouldn't have jumped ass-first into a situation you couldn't handle."

"I was handling it; Digger escaped."

"Be careful another mistake like that doesn't happen again, King. It could be the last one you ever make."

"Are you threatening me?" His eyes narrowed on her.

Evie sighed. "I'm only going to tell you once; don't ever grab me again like you did just now. No one touches me without permission, and you sure as fuck don't have it."

"You're the one who attempted to slap me for insulting you."

"I didn't try to slap you for insulting me. I tried to slap you for insulting Beth and Lily. They're your daughter and cousin. You should have enough respect for them not to ask stupid questions like you just did. They are both in committed relationships, and they are completely faithful to each other. I, on the other hand, can fuck anyone I want."

"Is that an invitation?"

"Are you that lame? No, it wasn't an invitation; I would never fuck a man like you." Evie made no effort to hide her disgust.

"I would never fuck you, either. I could catch something." His contempt drilled a hole through her heart.

Evie jumped out of the way just in time to dodge the fist Lucky aimed at King. King staggered back, but before he was able to catch his balance, Lucky was on him, trying to pound him into the ground. King swung back, managing to knock Lucky off; however, Lucky managed to hit him in the chest where his gunshot wound was located. King lay back on the ground with Lucky hitting him even harder.

Evie tried to pull Lucky off but couldn't budge him. A pair of hands moved her out of the way before reaching down to pull Lucky off King. When Lucky would have attacked Henry, Evie grabbed him around the waist, holding on tight.

"Stop it, Lucky," she called out.

He stopped trying to get loose, staring at King with deadly eyes as King was helped to his feet. Blood was showing through the material of his shirt. Evie started to reach out to check him when he fell back to the ground.

"King!"

Lily ran to her father with Shade on her heels, glancing up quickly at Lucky and Evie with accusing eyes.

Evie looked King over carefully and realized they had played right into King's hand. They had been had by a card shark.

Chapter Seven

"How is he?" Evie asked as Beth and Lily came into the clubhouse. She had parked her ass on one of the barstools in the clubroom and was nursing a glass of whiskey while she waited for them to come back.

"Better. A stitch broke loose, but it looked worse than it was." Neither Beth nor Lily looked at her accusingly any longer, yet the tense silence between them was telling.

Evie picked up her glass and took a drink. "Do you want to know what happened?"

"Beth and I talked about it on the way home," Lily said. "We want to apologize for King's behavior. I wasn't aware he was being rude to you, or I would never have gone to his house for dinner."

Evie set her glass down on the counter. "He told you what he said to me?"

"No, he refused to talk about it. I told him if he continued to be rude to my friends, I would no longer see him."

"So, how did you know what he said to me?"

"I didn't. I saw you both arguing when I came out of the church store, and I could tell from your face it was something bad when Pastor Dean—I mean, Lucky—jumped him. After Beth said he looked worse than he was, it didn't take much to figure out he's trying to place a wedge between me and The Last Riders."

Evie had to give Lily props; she had figured out King's game. It was only when Evie had seen King's eyes flicker in Lily's direction that she had figured it out.

"Anyways, Shade and I leave Monday for Alaska and King will go back to Queen City, so everything will go back to normal then," Lily said optimistically while ignoring both Evie and Beth's dubious looks.

Evie downed the rest of her drink after the two women went to bed. She then poured herself another, planning on getting shit-faced and fucked. Since she would be going back with Penni on Monday, also, she would be doing without until she came back.

Evie stared around the clubhouse room, seeing Train and Cash playing cards. Lucky had already gone upstairs with Bliss to work off his aggression. Rider was sitting on the couch with Stori who had Nickel on the other side. Several other brothers were lounging around the two sofas at the end of the room.

Evie finished her drink, standing up languidly.

"Who won?"

"I did," Cash said, showing his cards.

"Feel like playing again?"

"Yes. So, what are we playing for? "

Evie watched as he shuffled the cards.

"The winner gets to be on top."

* * *

King stood at his window smoking his cigar. He had fucked up. He had made his move too soon, underestimating Lily seeing through him. He should have known he couldn't fake being hurt. Hell, he could have taken a worse beating than that with three gunshot wounds.

His fingers rubbed his eyes tiredly. He never felt bad

about any shit he pulled, but tonight, his conscience was riding him hard. Lily wasn't the source of his guilt, though; she didn't realize what she was caught up in. The source of his guilt was Evie.

He had never manhandled a woman before, and it didn't sit well with him now. He hadn't done anything other than grab her arm, yet it had been out of line and he knew it.

He chewed on the end of his cigar as he thought about her expression when he had said he could catch something from her. She had tried to hide the hurt he had inflicted.

He had deliberately started the argument outside when Lily had texted him she was about to leave the store. He had ruthlessly used Evie to set The Last Riders up when he had seen Lucky go outside after Willa. He was becoming an expert at sparking Evie's temper, so he had said the most hurtful thing he could say to her and waited for the fireworks. Everything had gone the way he had planned except for his own reaction to the hurt in Evie's eyes.

Lily and Shade were leaving on Monday and so would he. He would use that time to find a way to destroy The Last Riders. Then, when Lily returned, he would fly back to Kentucky.

He stared out at the dark mountains, wondering whose bed Evie was in tonight. He had a variety of sexual partners at his beck and call. He usually went for the petite women. He wasn't attracted to women with attitudes, nor did he like his women taking a dip in someone else's pool. Evie was the exact opposite of everything he wanted; tall with brown hair that had highlights of red and gold, whiskey-colored eyes, and a body that was firm and lithe. She reminded him of an expensive glass of bourbon with all the hidden delights and a strong bite.

King bit down on his cigar. After his stunt today, his seduction was going to take time. Jackal had called earlier in the day to inform him Evie was accompanying Penni back to Queen City. A member's wife from Jackal's biker club was friends with Penni; therefore, the information had come as no shock to him. The Last Riders were checking on him.

His life was one of violence. He held a stranglehold on Queen City. No illegal activity happened in his city without his permission and a cut of the profits. All those who tried found themselves out of the city or six-feet under. The last few years had been calm since, over the years, no one had dared to challenge his authority except Digger who was now in protective custody, courtesy of the state of Texas.

"Should you be out of bed?"

King didn't let his surprise show. He didn't even bother to turn around, instead looking at his son-in-law's reflection in the glass. "I needed to move around. You just missed Lily and Beth."

"I saw them leave."

King took a deep draw of his cigar. "Henry okay?"

"He'll wake up in a few minutes."

King turned to face Shade. "Say what you want to say."

"Stop, King. Go back to Queen City. Live your life. If you want to play father, call Lily once a month. Come and see her for a week in the summer. But stay out of our lives the rest of the time."

"And if I don't? I'm not someone you can make disappear without Lily asking questions."

"I don't have to make you disappear, King." Shade's eyes held the promise while his features remained emotionless.

"I see, like how the two bikers who nearly killed Lily ended up at the bottom of Black Mountain?"

Shade's stony silence filled the room. King had met every type of man imaginable in his type of work; however, this man staring at him from across the room was different. He didn't react with anger at his manipulations or cutting remarks. Nothing got beneath his skin. He was as cold-blooded as a snake, and sooner or later, he would strike out and hurt Lily. King's stomach clenched with fury that his daughter was married to the sinister assassin.

An ironic smile came to Shade's lips. "I understand your desire to protect Lily from me, but I will never hurt Lily—I would die for her. You, on the other hand, have always placed your own needs above hers. You were the one who left her in the care of a mother who sold her. You were the one who placed a child molester in her home. And you were the one who nearly got her killed three weeks ago. Lily needs protection from only one person—you."

King crushed his cigar out. "You don't need to remind me of the mistakes I've made with her. I plan to do better by her."

"The only way you can do better is by staying out of her life. You're not going to fix your past mistakes now. It's too late." Shade went to the bedroom door.

"You're not going to keep me out of her life. You're wrong for her, and we both know it. When I prove it to her, she'll leave you behind. You don't frighten me, Shade. It's been awhile since I've had to get my hands dirty, but that doesn't mean I've forgotten how."

"Go home, King." When Shade went out the door as quietly as he'd entered, King went out after him, but he was already gone. He found Henry lying on the kitchen floor, just coming to.

"What in the fuck happened?" he asked as King helped him to his feet.

Damn, I'm getting old, he thought as he felt his body's aches and pains under Henry's staggering weight. "Shade."

"Damn, I didn't even hear him."

"I didn't either until he talked."

"I think you're biting off more than you can chew with him, Boss." Henry's cautionary words weren't a deterrent, but he wasn't stupid either. He hadn't lived this long being stupid.

"Next time, I'll be more careful."

"If you're not, I don't think either of us will be alive to regret it."

Chapter Eight

Penni tossed her magazine down on the couch between them. "Let's go out to dinner. I'm bored sitting around the apartment."

Evie looked at Shade's sister in amusement. "We've only been back two days."

She shrugged. "I know, but I want to go out." She leaned forward, looking at her with her pleading blue eyes. "Please, Evie… please."

Evie playfully shoved her off the couch. "Okay, okay. Jeez."

The women grabbed their jackets before going out the door. Penni's apartment was close to several of the higher-end restaurants, but they chose a restaurant that was more laid back, deciding to sit outside at one of the small tables.

They were discussing how much Penni was looking forward to going back to work the next week when a dark car pulled up to the restaurant across the street. Evie recognized the man getting out of the driver's side door.

Henry walked around the front of the car, opening the back door. King came out, reaching his hand back in for the beautiful woman sliding out of the car with a seductive smile aimed at an elegant King dressed in an expensive dark suit. King's arm circled the woman's waist as he escorted her inside the expensive restaurant.

The woman's pale-pink ice dress moved fluidly against her body as she walked. The dress was stunning, the flowing silk ending just below her knees with a row of ruffles. Evie had last worn ruffles when she was five-years-old. On King's date, they looked flirty and enticing. She was everything Evie had turned her back on years ago.

Evie took a long drink of her beer.

"Something wrong?" Penni asked at her sudden silence.

"No. You ready to go?" Evie paid the check.

Walking back to the apartment building, she listened to Penni's enthusiasm, which brought back her own reflections of how long it had been since she had felt the same about her own job.

She loved being around The Last Riders. She even enjoyed the laid-back lifestyle of working in the factory. However, she was a NP and that was being ignored. She was going to use the time she was in Queen City to come to some hard decisions she had been avoiding.

* * *

"She's here."

King sat at his table doing paperwork. At Henry's words, his eyes went to the doorway, seeing Evie walking through as if she went to a strip show every Saturday night.

He had wondered when she would show up. She had been in Queen City for over a week. Jackal had told him she and Penni had driven there from Treepoint while he had flown home. He had been confident she would show up at his strip club; how else was she supposed to find out what she needed to know?

Shade would want to know if Lily was in danger. How else would he do that other than to send someone in to find out? The sexy woman was the perfect one, too. His son-in-law was a smart bastard.

King had no intention of getting Lily hurt. In fact, he had decided to get out of the business, but the man he wanted to take over was proving resistant. Until he came around, King was unable to move on. He had fought for years to reach the position he was in, yet now, he couldn't give it away fast enough.

"Tell Jackal I have another job for him. I want him to get Evie's background. I have a feeling I'm going to need all the help I can get." Henry moved away to follow his order while King looked Evie over as she took a seat not far from the stage, and one of his girls took her drink order.

Women would often come in to watch the shows, usually with their boyfriends or husbands, wanting them to get horny enough to climb into bed together. *I doubt Evie has that problem*, he thought cynically. She sat at the table confidently, ignoring the admiring gazes of the rowdy men sitting around her.

King lit a cigar, studying her as she drank her drink and watched Sherri on the stage. She even whistled a couple of times, yelling encouragement when Sherri almost tripped as she finished her spin before she had regained her equilibrium.

King signaled to Henry, who had come back after his call to Jackal. "Tell Sherri, if she doesn't pass the next drug test, she's gone. I've warned her about taking something before she gets on the stage."

"She says she needs it to get on the stage." Henry's defense of the woman came as no surprise.

"She won't need it if there isn't a stage to get on. You can tell she's high."

"I'll talk to her." Henry withdrew at his sharp gaze. He was getting fucking tired of Sherri taking advantage of being his headliner.

King went back to observing Evie, who was ignoring him. He got up from his table, walking across the room. Usually, he sent for the ones he wanted to talk to and had someone bring them to his table. He was sure Evie would ignore the order, however.

When he pulled out a chair at her table and took a seat, she didn't say anything.

"How are you enjoying the show?" King was amused at her pretended indifference to his presence.

Evie looked at him briefly before lifting her drink. "Are your girls always stoned?"

King's mouth tightened. "No, usually I fire them."

As Evie finished her drink, King motioned for Angel to bring her another.

"How are you enjoying staying with Penni?"

Evie's face lit with affection. "You can't *not* enjoy being around that girl. She's in a perpetual good mood."

"I don't think Jackal would agree with you." Her indifference disappeared at his sardonic comment.

"The fucker who kidnapped her?"

"He didn't exactly kidnap her; he held her as collateral for one of his friends," King reasoned.

"I think Penni would disagree with you."

"He won't be bothering her again."

"No, he won't." Evie's quick agreement had King wondering what measures she had taken to ensure Jackal wasn't allowed another opportunity to get near Penni.

"If he fucks with her again, he might get more than he bargained for." Her smug smile had King thinking he should pass on a small warning to the biker.

When Angel set Evie's drink down in front of her, managing to rub her breasts against King's shoulder as she leaned over, Evie caught the movement with amusement.

"I don't fuck my girls." King interpreted her look.

"I don't care who you fuck." Her steady gaze didn't shy away from his.

"You don't mind sharing?"

"Never have, never will."

"That's a dangerous concept."

She leaned forward, putting her face in his. "I know

you're old," her insult struck a nerve, "but there is such a thing as condoms. I'm not the one who doesn't practice safe sex."

"I'm not old. I'm only forty-three."

Sherri finished her set, leaving the stage.

"When's the next show?" Evie faked a yawn.

"Fifteen minutes. Do you want me to show you around the club?" King offered, trying to regroup. He couldn't seduce the woman if she hated his guts; he was actually going to have to work hard to get Evie to drop her guard. It was his own fault; so far, he had been the mastermind of fuckups.

Evie shrugged. "I don't have anything better to do for fifteen minutes."

King stood up, leading the way through the club. He took her backstage to the dressing area where he opened the girls' dressing room without knocking. Sherri was getting dressed, and a new girl he had hired just a few weeks ago was sliding her panties on. Both women were naked from the waist up.

"King!" Pepper squealed. The girl dropped the top she was about to put on to run to him, pressing her bared breasts against his chest as she reached up to kiss him. King let her have his mouth for a second before raising his head, stepping back and taking her wrists in his hands to move her hands away.

"Sherri, Pepper, this is Evie."

Both women studied Evie, sizing her up as competition on the stage, and their friendly looks disappeared. King could understand why, too. Evie looked sexy in tight jeans that hugged her ass, a wine-colored t-shirt leaving the tops of her breasts bare, and her black leather boots coming up to her thighs. Around her throat was a black leather collar that had silver studs.

King's eyes roved over her. She had an air of confidence usually found only in men. He was becoming more and more attracted to her each time he was in her presence. If she wasn't The Last Riders' whore, he would have already made a move to fuck her himself.

"You going to work for King?" Pepper asked, sliding on her see-through, white angel top then putting on the fake wings.

"No. I only strip in private."

"Oh, you're a private contractor. I did that once and was dumb enough to do a bachelor party. After that, I went to work for King."

"I'll make sure not to take any bachelor parties."

When a knock came at the door, Pepper grinned before going to open it. "I'm up."

After the door closed behind her, Sherri took a step forward. "Sorry, King. Henry told me what you said. I'll make sure I don't do it again."

"You want to do that shit, do it on your own time, not mine. If you need to take something to get on the stage, I can put you on serving drinks."

"No. The money's not as good."

"Then don't screw up again," he warned without sympathy.

"I won't."

King led Evie out of the dressing room and back out front.

"What's up there?" She motioned to the steps that led upstairs.

"I'll show you."

The stairway had gold carpeting and led to a large, gold door. King pressed a button and it automatically opened. He watched Evie's reaction when she entered the VIP room. It was busy tonight with a large crowd.

He showed her to a booth at the back of the room, motioning for her to slide in. She slipped in, scooting over so he could sit down on the circular seat.

King made sure he slid close enough to her that his thigh and shoulder brushed hers.

"Hi, King. What can I get you two?"

"Bring us two of the Dalmore 62." He saw Evie's amused expression. "What's so funny?"

"You and Shade have a lot in common."

"Really, I don't think we're anything alike." King's mouth tightened at the thought of his son-in-law.

Evie burst out laughing as Ashley set the glasses of expensive whiskey down in front of them. "If you didn't have a stick up your ass where he's concerned, you could be best friends." She took a drink of the whiskey.

Her glistening lips were more than he could resist. He leaned down, catching her mouth with his own.

Evie jerked her mouth away from his. "Stop flirting with me, King."

"Why? I think you're sexy as hell."

"You also think I'm a whore." She downed her drink when he remained quiet. "You're a real bastard."

"Yes, but since when did you only fuck nice guys?" King snapped his mouth closed. He couldn't keep from antagonizing the woman. Her fiery spirit gave him a respite from the ennui he had been experiencing for the last year.

She leaned closer to him, her hand running up the length of his thigh under the table. His cock jerked in lust, thickening behind his suit's pants as her fingers traced over the outline before cupping it in her hand.

"I've known men like you my whole life. Men who think only a man deserves sexual satisfaction. Even those goody-two-shoes bitches who see me on the back of one of the men's bikes will call me slut because it's too mortifying to admit even to themselves that I'm getting laid and enjoying every minute of it. I'm fairly young and having fun. I play with people who feel the same, just wanting our freedom. There's nothing wrong with that, is there?"

King shook his head no, gritting his teeth in pain because her hand had tightened on each word until his cock was clutched in a grip that threatened to break his composure. "I see your point."

"I hope you do," Evie said, releasing his cock to pick up her drink.

"Have you eaten? You're going to get sick with that on an empty stomach."

"I had dinner before I came. Besides, it'll take more than three glasses of whiskey to get me drunk."

"Good."

"Why?"

"Because I don't fuck a woman when she's drunk."

"I'm not going to fuck you," she snapped. "I don't even like you!"

"You like everyone you ever fucked?"

"Yes."

"Then I'll be the first," King said, finishing his drink. "Let me show you the rest of the club."

He thought for a minute she would refuse, but she slid out of the booth. King moved to the side of the room where windows looked into the private rooms and pulled Evie closer for a better look. Inside the room, Jazz was giving a lap dance.

The sultry dancer was standing over the client with a leg on the side of his chair while she ground her breasts into his chest. Her ass was swaying to the beat of the music King and Evie couldn't hear.

"The room is soundproof," he offered, seeing the question in her eyes.

Jazz straightened imperceptibly, raising her arms to place behind her head. She lifted and tossed her hair around as her breasts, covered only in a small pasty at her nipples, swung in front of his mouth.

"Why is the other curtain pulled over that room?" Evie pointed to the room next to the one they were looking through.

"The client wanted privacy." The red room had a separate entrance from downstairs that the client was given a special key to. The lap dancer was given a door code only she knew at the time of the appointment. The dances involved no clothes on the dancer and touching was allowed, of course. The dancer's fee skyrocketed at the added services. The elite in town didn't mind paying his prices for their privacy, though.

"Let me show you my other rooms." King took her arm, walking her across the crowded floor where there was a set of three doors. King keyed in a number, opening the door in the middle and allowing Evie to go first. His hand on her back gave her a gentle nudge forward.

"I've got it, Trey. Take a break." The large man who provided security stood up from the stool he was sitting on and left the room. King leaned back against the wall, studying Evie as she took in what was going on in the two rooms.

The room they were standing in was the size of a large closet. There were two doors that each led into the two separate rooms. King was sure it was what was going on in the two rooms that had her mouth dropping open; each opulent bedroom had occupants having sex. King crossed his arms over his chest as he watched her reaction.

A feral grin came to his lips when he saw her nipples tighten and she shifted her weight. Her unconscious movements aroused King's predatory instincts.

"Is this supposed to turn me on?" Evie turned back to face him, taking him by complete surprise. "Sorry, I don't get turned on by women getting paid to take it up the ass. Nor being paid to pretend to be a high schooler." Her eyes narrowed on his. "She is pretending, isn't she?"

"Of course, I don't deal in kids. What kind of man do you take me for?"

"Someone who would make a dime off someone taking it up the ass," she replied sarcastically.

When King came off the wall with lethal intent, her eyes widened. The bitch had finally realized she had pushed him too far.

"For your information, the one being paid in that room is Rory, not the woman. She's a housewife who's not getting what she needs from her tight-assed husband.

"It's taken me several years to work out a system that benefits my clients and my workers. They don't walk the streets or get hurt by someone because that's how that sicko gets off. I provide safe, monitored rooms that are clean and clients are checked out before they are even touched. So I take my cut? It's a lot less than anyone else would take, and they don't have to worry if they'll still be breathing afterward."

Evie didn't apologize for her harsh words, but she lost the accusing look from her eyes.

King's hand went to the back of her neck, bringing her to his chest. "Everyone should be allowed to fulfill their fantasy." His lips traced across the line of her jaw until he came to her mouth, taking it with his. Her lips parted under the pressure and he took advantage, his tongue sliding into the silky warmth of her mouth. She tasted like the expensive whiskey she had just drunk.

King groaned, leaning into her further, bracing his weight with a hand on the wall behind her. He again took advantage of her hesitation, controlling the kiss, using years of experience with women to raise her desire. When he smelled the sweet scent of her arousal, he took his mouth away, tracing his mouth to the delicate shell of her ear. "What's your fantasy, Evie?"

Chapter Nine

Evie put her hands on his chest, giving herself breathing room. "I don't have one."

"Everyone has a fantasy."

"I don't. I keep my feet planted in reality." Evie moved away from his touch, going out the door without waiting.

"That can't be much fun." King came up from behind her, taking her arm.

"It's time I left."

"I'll give you a ride."

"I'm going to leave the same way I came—in a taxi." Evie refused his offer, not wanting to spend any more time with him until she could rebuild her guard.

King took his phone out of his pocket while leading her to the door of the VIP room. "Bring the car to the front."

Evie came to a sudden stop. "I told you I was taking a taxi."

"It's late, and it will take at least thirty minutes for one to get here. Surely, me giving you a ride to Penni's won't take that long. Either way, you're going to be stuck with my company."

Evie sighed, seeing she wasn't going to win this particular battle. "Okay." Evie figured the quickest way to get away from him was accepting a ride.

They went out the front door of the strip club where his black car was already waiting. King opened the door for her and Evie slid inside the car, sinking back against the expensive leather.

As Henry pulled out into the light traffic, Evie looked out the darkened window. The lights from the tall buildings were beautiful. Treepoint was small; the tallest building there might be seven stories compared to the skyscrapers reaching toward the sky here.

"It's been so long since I was in a big city I forgot what it was like," Evie murmured.

"Which city did you live in?"

Evie didn't answer his question.

"What are you doing tomorrow night?"

Evie turned back to him. "Nothing, why?"

"I'm going to a dinner party, and I want you to come with me."

Evie started to refuse then changed her mind. If she was going to find out what she needed to know for Shade, then she needed to see all aspects of his life, both business and personal.

"I can do that," Evie replied as if it was no big deal. "Do you need Penni's address?"

"No, Henry already knows it."

Evie wasn't surprised. From the information she had already gathered in the past week, there wasn't much King didn't know that went on in Queen City.

Five minutes later, his car slid to a stop in front of Penni's apartment building. Henry got out and opened the door for her.

"Goodnight, King."

"Goodnight, Evie." His mocking reply had her wanting to tell him to go fuck himself; instead, she bit back her caustic reply and slid out of the car.

Penni's apartment building was the most secure in the city. Shade had paid for it, making her switch from the one Jackal had kidnapped her out of.

As the doorman let her in, she thanked him, seeing the curious gleam in his eyes as he watched King's car drive away.

Afterward, the nosy fucker gave her what couldn't be a more gracious smile as he pushed the elevator button for her. Evie was relieved when the doors opened. Forcing herself to be polite, she tipped him before going inside.

Penni was already in bed when Evie let herself in the apartment. Shade had rented Penni a two-bedroom, so Evie went to the bedroom she was staying in. Showering, she got ready for bed, brushing her hair and sliding on one of Rider's t-shirts.

Feeling melancholy, she went to her bed, pulling out the gold chain with a locket she wore infrequently now. When Levi had died, she had worn it all the time, never taking it off. Gradually over the last few years, she had placed it in her jewelry box, only wearing it when she had felt his memory slipping away.

Pressing down, she opened the locket and took out the ring it concealed. Looking down at it, she felt a lump in her throat, battling down the excruciating pain in her chest she felt each time she looked at the diamond. Lying down on the bed, she held the ring in her hand, rubbing her thumb repeatedly over it.

Nights like this were when she would climb into bed with one of the members and let them take all the heartache away so she would finally be exhausted enough to sleep. Some nights, it would take a couple of them and several glasses of alcohol to drive the pain away and send her into a sleep where she could forget for a few peaceful hours.

Sighing, she got out of the bed; she wasn't going to be able to sleep anytime soon. She opened the curtains, taking a chair and pulling it to the window, curling up on it as she stared into the inky darkness with a thousand glittering lights. She stayed at the window long enough to see most of the lights go off as the city fell asleep while she remained wide-awake, reliving her past.

* * *

"You look tired tonight."

"I never sleep well when I'm away from the club." She almost put a hand to her face at his comment, but forced herself to appear relaxed.

Evie waited for King to make a nasty comment and was relieved when he didn't. She was too tired to fence with him tonight.

King's car pulled up to a large mansion and Evie raised a brow at it, whistling softly. "It's a good thing I dressed up."

"You look beautiful," King said, getting out of the car behind her.

"First, I look tired, and now I'm beautiful. You need to make up your mind."

King's head tilted to the side as he stared down at her. "You look both; beautiful with a touch of vulnerability. It suits you."

The mansion was filled with people. Evie wasn't intimated, however, as she was escorted through the crowded room by King who came to a stop in front of a middle-aged couple.

"Evie, I'd like to introduce you to Desmond Beck and Marta Lewis."

She shook both of their hands as King made the introductions. Evie could tell from one look at his eyes as they traveled over her body that Desmond Beck was a rich, elegant and cold bastard. Marta, on the other hand, was sugary-sweet and didn't have two brain cells that connected. Her breasts were larger than her IQ.

Evie was forced to listen to her discuss her latest pedicure as King and Desmond talked about their investment in a building. She listened as they talked about the new leases they had signed while pretending to pay attention to Marta move on to her hairdresser getting married and how painful it was to find a new one.

Thankfully, it wasn't long before dinner was served and Evie was finally able to move away from Marta.

"If you don't get her away from me, I'm going to scream," Evie threatened in a low voice.

"You don't like her?"

"A five-year-old would get along with her better than I would."

King laughed as he pulled a chair out for her. Evie sat down at the elegant table, studying the people already seated around it. King had surrounded himself with the upper class. From what Shade had told her, King had been dirt poor when he was raised and now had accumulated enough money to move in higher circles. She was disappointed that he fit the cliché of wanting to rub people's noses in his wealth.

She took a drink of the expensive wine, not enjoying the taste—Evie had never been much of a wine drinker. Setting her wine glass down, she picked up her water glass instead.

"You don't like the wine?" Her host, Desmond, lifted an inquiring brow.

"The wine is fine. I just don't care for it."

"Let me guess, your drink of choice is whiskey?"

"I like anything with a kick to it, but if it comes down to just one, I'm just as content with a beer." Evie picked up her salad fork, ignoring his amused laughter.

"To tell you the truth, so do I." Desmond motioned for the server. "Bring us two beers. King?"

"No, thanks. I'll stick to the wine."

Evie took a bite of her salad, hating it. God, she didn't miss the days of having to choke down pretentious food made to look prettier than it actually tasted.

When the server set their beers down, Evie politely uttered her thanks.

"You're welcome." Desmond smiled graciously. "So, how did you meet King?"

Evie quit pretending to eat her salad. "I met him while he was on vacation." Evie deliberately didn't mention Lily.

"Where did you go on vacation, King?"

"Kentucky."

"Kentucky?"

"Yes."

"That's an interesting spot. I'm afraid I don't know much about Kentucky," Desmond mused.

"It's beautiful. The mountains, horses and people are worth giving it a visit," Evie stated.

"I'll keep that in mind. Is that where you're from?"

"No, it's where I live now. I'm originally from Atlanta."

"A big-city girl going to a small town. That was a big change."

"Not really. The adjustment came when I joined the military."

"You served overseas?"

"Yes." Before he could ask another question, Evie asked one of her own. "You and King are business partners?"

"Yes, we grew up together." That did surprise Evie. She had to take back her original assessment of King kissing up to money. However, it had been an easy assumption to make when King's harsh features bore the signs of his hard upbringing while the man she was seated next to was elegant and refined. "It's been a very lucrative partnership. I let King handle the business, and I reap all the benefits."

Evie heard King's amused laughter. "Don't sell yourself short, Desmond. You more than carry your own weight."

Desmond lifted his beer to King.

The next course was much more edible as Evie was able to manage the veal chops. Then, forgoing the designer ice cream, she enjoyed the fruit plate for dessert.

Desmond escorted her from the dinner table with King

following behind. Marta, who was not happy, had lost the friendly attitude she had greeted her with.

Seating Evie on a chair, Desmond turned to King. "Bring her around again. Your taste is getting better." He turned to Evie. "I need to circulate. It was nice meeting you, Evie. Come to lunch before you go back to Kentucky."

"I don't know how long I'm staying." She prevaricated.

"Perhaps King can lure you away from small-town living. A large city does have its advantages."

"So does a small town. At least we grow them smart there." She looked at Marta, who was impatiently pulling at his sleeve.

"Touché," he said, giving her a wry smile before moving away.

"That wasn't nice," King said, sitting down casually on the arm of her chair.

"I know, and I'm deeply ashamed of myself." She wasn't and never would be. Women like Marta were her pet peeve. No one could be that stupid. The woman had deliberately dumbed herself down and had her breasts enlarged a couple of sizes to catch herself a rich lover.

"You ready to go?"

"Yes." She rose to her feet, anxious to get away from the snobs who had been obviously scrutinizing her all evening.

King escorted her outside where Henry was waiting with the car door open.

"It's a thing with him, isn't it?" Evie asked as soon as King closed the car door.

"What is?"

"Opening and closing doors."

"It's his job," King said, leaning back in the dark car.

Evie didn't talk on the way back to Penni's apartment. When the door opened, she was about to get out when she realized they weren't at Penni's.

"Where are we?"

"My penthouse. I thought we would have a nightcap."

Evie almost didn't get out. Only the thought of another sleepless night had her following him up.

She would take a drink or two then leave. There wasn't a chance anything else would happen. He was Lily's father, and she was here to find out if he was a danger to her. More importantly, she wasn't even attracted to him. What could go wrong?

Chapter Ten

Evie entered his penthouse suite, amazed at the size of the living room.

"Wow." She didn't hide her reaction; the room deserved all the props she could give it. Decorated similarly to his house in Treepoint with black leather couches and glass tables, it fit the room much more than it ever would the small house. The modern furnishing blended with the architecture in the building with a wall of windows that spanned the whole room.

Evie went directly to the windows to gaze out. "This is fantastic."

"Do you want a drink?"

"Yes, please."

Evie turned from the window, going to the couch. Kicking off her high heels, she sat down, curling her feet under her.

"Make yourself at home," he said, sitting down next to her and handing her a drink.

"My feet were killing me. It's been a long time since I wore heels that tall," Evie admitted.

"I would never have known," King replied. "How did

you end up with The Last Riders? You obviously have a background where you're used to money."

"I still have money. I just don't choose to spend it on expensive apartments," Evie commented, her hand waving around the room. "This is beautiful but artificial."

"Did you just insult me?" King set his glass down on the table, placing his arm on the back of the sofa behind her. "What do you spend your money on? Clothes?" His fingers lifted the material of her dress, running it between his fingers.

"Among other things."

"Do you make a lot of money, filling factory orders?"

"That was a crass comment, besides being out of line."

"I've never had a problem with what people thought of me."

"I bet you don't have many friends, do you?"

"No, Desmond and Henry are pretty much it. Yet, I'd like to count you as a friend, Evie. I think we have a lot in common."

"We have nothing in common."

"You don't think so? I do. I think both of us are emotional misfits. You can go from man to man without leaving your heart behind. I can go from woman to woman without them touching mine. We're a match made in Heaven."

"Or Hell," Evie said under her breath, setting her own glass down. "King, I need to set you straight before this goes any further. You can stop flirting with me. You're not going to succeed in seducing me."

"Why not? You're attracted to me."

Evie thought about denying it but decided to be truthful. "You're a very attractive man. Despite that, I've already given you my reasons."

"Why? Because I'm Lily's father?"

"Yes."

"Why would that make you feel uncomfortable when you've slept with her husband?"

Picking up her drink, she finished the contents before setting it back down. "You're unbelievable."

Evie took a deep breath. "Shade and I met in high school. I've told you this before. Razer, Lucky and Knox were in the service together, stationed at the same military base. We hung out together on the weekends."

Evie could tell he was about to make a smart-ass comment; if he did, she was out of here. Shade could have him. Luckily, he remained quiet.

"We were friends. We were sent in after the fighting to clean up after everyone else's mess and get out the causalities. They had started to pull Shade for special assignments, and when they did, they would send in Cash. That's how we met Viper and Gavin. They were in another unit.

"I was young, dumb, and God, so idealistic." Evie shook her head at her naivety even now.

Getting up, she took her glass to the bar, pouring herself another drink. Instead of sitting back down, she leaned against the bar, facing him and keeping the bottle near.

"It's not easy for a woman to be in the military. There's a lot of sexism. I had several brushes with it, but I was fortunate to have friends who always watched out for me. I was six weeks from getting out when a Corpsman at base camp was injured by enemy fire and was medavaced to the base hospital. They needed someone immediately, as a result I was ordered to the new unit. Most of the men there had been in country longer, and for many of them, it was their second or third tour. The unit commander should have been released from duty. It was like a sociopath over a pack of wild dogs. I thought I could handle him. He was from Atlanta and had casually dated my sister for a short time when he was on leave."

She was still looking at King, but she was no longer seeing him, her mind going back to the past. "One night, we had come back from a skirmish. The adrenaline was high and the men were antsy. It made me nervous to just be around them, so I went to my quarters. I didn't even take the time for a shower. I called Shade to check in with him and the others, and he could tell from my voice that something was wrong, that I was scared. He told me to stay put and he would come as soon as he got permission from his unit commander.

"I hung up from him, and for about ten seconds, I felt better, believed I was just imagining the men were losing control. Then I heard the knock on my door. I didn't answer, but it didn't matter. Four men broke it down. One was my unit commander. They laughed at me when I tried to fight them off. Made fun of me for entering the military, asking me why I had joined if I didn't want a steady supply of dick." Evie picked up her glass, taking a large drink.

"By the time Shade found me the next morning, they had made me their personal toy. When Shade walked in and saw what had happened, he did what I wished I could have done. It took six men to get him off them.

"You're going to enjoy this part." She lifted her glass at King.

"I'm not enjoying any part of this." King had been given a basic bio on Evie by Jackal. He seemed to have left out quite a bit of pertinent information.

"Shade was the one brought up on charges. It was a mess. All the surrounding units knew the stories. Anytime I was around them, they called me some of the vilest names imaginable. The men said I had led them on, had let them in my room. I had two broken ribs, one had punched me in the eye, and I had a dislocated shoulder."

"Damn."

Evie took another drink. "They moved me back to my original unit, though. If not for Shade, I don't know what I would have done. We would sit and talk for hours while he listened to me rant and rave. Four weeks later, I was discharged. So, when you throw Shade up to me, it really pisses me off. Lily is lucky he loves her. She couldn't be in safer hands."

King got up from the sofa, coming to stand next to her, sliding his hand under the thick swathe of her hair. "What happened to the men?"

"They were killed by enemy fire the next week. The whole unit was nearly wiped out. If they hadn't raped me, then I would have been with them and killed."

"You don't know that for sure."

"Yes, I do. Knox's wife was my replacement. She was killed in my place."

"God."

"I don't know if Knox would agree with you, but it was bad. They had only been married a short while."

"He's the sheriff of Treepoint?"

"Yes, he's married to Diamond. I'm glad he fell in love again."

"So, you joined The Last Riders when you got out of the service?"

Evie was done talking about the past. "Send for Henry. I'm ready to go home."

"Stay." King used his hand on the back of her neck to pull her closer. Before she could say anything, he caught her mouth with his. His other arm wrapped around her waist, pulling her close to his warm body. She was chilled from recounting the past.

Evie didn't want to go back to her empty bed and stay another night wide-awake, remembering the past. She needed to forget, and she had a willing male to help make her. Letting her weight sink into his, her mouth gave her answer.

King lifted her up, carrying her down a dark hallway into his bedroom, not bothering to turn on the lights. Setting her down on the mattress, his hands went under her dress to pull down her stockings. Evie wiggled her hips, helping him as she raised her arms to pull off her dress.

She sat on the side of his bed, completely naked except

for the tiny bra covering her breasts. Her hands then went to the clasp on the front, but King beat her to it, unsnapping it with a flick of his fingers.

His expressionless face swiftly turned to one of lust. He jerked his shirt off, snapping several of the buttons as he toed off his shoes. Evie bent forward, unbuckling his trousers and unzipping them, pulling out his cock.

Evie gave a murmur of approval. "Not bad for an old man." Damn, a younger man in his twenties would be envious of the erection she held in her hand. Unable to resist, she scooted to the edge of the bed, taking his cock in her mouth.

"Fuck," King hissed.

Evie smiled against him as she took him to the back of her throat in an experienced move she had perfected long ago. Her fingers pulled him out of his pants farther to be able to reach more of him. She felt King sliding his pants down and kicking them away without budging his cock from her greedy mouth. Her tongue slid up and down his length as she took him to the back of her throat, swallowing against him.

His hands went to her hair, but he didn't try to push her down on him; instead, he used it to keep her steady as he began fucking her mouth. Her hand went to his balls, lifting the heavy sacs as she explored them while taking him even deeper.

Evie slid out of the bed, going to her knees on the floor. Taking her mouth off his cock, she went between his thighs to suck one ball, then the other into her mouth, her tongue lashing the tender flesh.

King used his hand in her hair to bring her back to his cock, guiding her back with his hand. "Open your mouth."

Evie willingly opened her mouth, letting him thrust back inside. She rubbed her breasts against his thighs, teasing her nipples as his thrusts sped up. Evie thought he was about to come; however, he had already lasted longer than she'd thought he would.

His hand pulled her hair as he jerked her head away from his cock, using it to make her stand. As he tossed her onto the bed, Evie panted, waiting to see what he was going to do next.

When King turned to the nightstand, Evie saw him pull out a condom, putting it on. She parted her thighs, her hand going between her legs as she stroked her clit. His face tensed as he watched her.

Reaching forward, he slapped her hand. Shocked, Evie removed her hand.

"This is mine until I'm done with it. That means no one touches it, pleasures it, but me. And that includes you."

Evie became angry. "Fuck off then."

"I'm going to get off in about ten minutes when I finish fucking that pussy of yours."

Evie started to argue but decided against it. Why start an argument over something he didn't mean anyway and she had no intention of obeying?

"Then get to it, or I'll let my fingers do the job."

King laughed. "The problem is you've forgotten how much going slow can build your orgasm."

"You're going to give me a lesson on fucking?"

"It will be one you will never forget."

Evie's head fell back on the mattress laughing, until King slammed his cock home in one thrust. Then, her laughter turned to a long moan as he began building her passion by tilting her pelvis up, his cock sliding against her g-spot with every hard thrust. His hand pressed down on her belly, making her shudder at the feel of him inside her. Damn, he knew how to fuck.

Evie wiggled her hips, trying to thrust against him, but he controlled her movements.

"I like having you underneath me, Evie. I like your tight pussy wrapped around my cock. Damn, it's hard to pick which one I want: to come in your pussy or your mouth."

"My pussy. I need to come," Evie threw in her vote.

"Are you always a greedy bitch when you fuck?"

"Yes, and I prefer doing it without all the chit-chat," she moaned.

King's hands tightened on her thighs, spreading her wider while his thumb brushed against her clit before sliding under the hood giving her the added friction she needed.

Evie felt her climax strike with waves of sensations that had her tossing on his bed, gripping his cock with her inner muscles. King groaned above her, pushing her legs up and pulling her hips closer, making her take every inch of his cock as he came.

When he finished, he pulled out then took off his condom, throwing it away in the trashcan beside the bed.

Evie tiredly closed her legs as she felt herself lifted and placed on the middle of the bed. The sex and alcohol she'd consumed were finally hitting her. With only a brief hour's sleep the night before, she was exhausted.

As King started to wake her up, she sensed he didn't want her to sleep in his bed, but she had no intention of getting up. She heard him picking up their clothes from the floor before going to the bathroom. As soon as the door closed, she climbed beneath the covers, snuggling down into the bed. Stretching out, she let her body relax on the silken sheets.

"He might never get me out of this bed." Her drowsy voice filled the oversized bedroom.

The bastard could fuck, so she might manage to have some fun in Queen City while she did what Shade wanted. No one said she couldn't find out everything she needed to know about King and still enjoy herself. If she could get him to lower his guard, she would be able to find out more about him while keeping her emotions contained. She was confident she could remain neutral. He didn't stand a shot in Hell of getting inside her heart—it was already taken.

Chapter Eleven

Sometime the next morning, a sharp smack on her ass woke her.

"Hey!" Evie mumbled, burrowing further under the pillow lying over the back of her head.

"I have to go to work."

"So? Go and leave me alone."

She felt the bed sink down next to her, his hand soothing the tingling on her ass before his mouth brushed her neck. "You owe me one."

Evie turned her head to the side, opening one eye. "If you've got the time, I've got the skill."

"Don't tempt me. I have a meeting in fifteen minutes; I've got to go. I'll send Henry back for you. He'll be downstairs when you're ready."

"Okay."

King's mouth kissed her lips briefly before he rose from the bed.

"King?"

"Yes?"

"Next time, leave me a note. Don't wake me up." She rolled over, sitting up in bed and rubbing her bleary eyes.

"I'll keep that in mind."

"Do that." She plopped backwards on the bed, pulling the pillow back over her face. "I'm on vacation, dammit."

His laughter followed him out the door as he slammed it behind him.

"Mother-fucker." She wouldn't be able to go back to sleep.

Taking her dress and underwear, she went into the bathroom where she showered and washed her hair; it didn't take long. Evie then stepped out of the shower, dressing quickly. Brushing her hair, she blow-dried it only long enough to take the wetness out, leaving it still damp.

Evie went into the bedroom, taking a deep breath and pushing the guilt down as she began her search.

* * *

"You want me to send Henry to get her?"

"No, leave her alone." King watched the security camera with his head of security. Taking a puff of his cigar, he stared at Evie as she searched through his drawers and closet. She even searched under his bed and mattress before going into the other room. The other room was treated the same before she put on her shoes and purse, going out the door without a backward glance.

"Call Henry and tell him she's on the way down, and put one of Jackal's men on her. I want her watched twenty-four hours unless she is with me."

"Got it."

King went out of the security room that was next-door to his office. Going to his desk, he opened the folder waiting for him; Jackal had handed it to him at their meeting. King drank his coffee while he read. When he finished, he sat back smoking his cigar. He should have checked her out before when he first realized he was attracted to her. He refused to feel guilty over some of the things he had said to her, though. How was he supposed to know she had been dealt a shitty hand?

King began wavering in his outright judgment on

Shade, as well. It was hard to judge them when his own life was much dirtier than theirs, and some of the things they had done were to right wrongs done to them.

Evie had been dealt with the worst. She had downplayed the viciousness she had suffered after her rape by the commanding officer. She had been a damn good Corpsman, and the Navy had lost a woman who'd had dreams of making the military a home. She had easily transferred her loyalty to The Last Riders, and King couldn't blame her.

He switched focus, bringing his mind back to work. He began making phone calls and taking appointments from those needing to be discreet. He also set up an important meeting with Ice. It took him the better part of the day before he could even take time to eat, and afterwards, before he went back to work, he called Evie.

"Hello?"

"Evie."

"How did you get my number?"

"I looked on your phone before I left."

"The phone was in my purse."

"Yes, it was." King couldn't hide the smile in his voice.

"Haven't you heard it's bad manners to snoop?" King thought that was hilarious coming from the woman who had searched through his underwear drawer.

"Sorry." He wasn't, just as he was sure she felt no recrimination for searching his apartment.

"What do you want?"

"Have dinner with me at the club."

"You want me to eat with you while women are on the stage naked?"

"Yes."

"Sounds like fun. What time?"

"Eight."

When she hung the phone up on him before he could say anything else, it actually made him smile. She was the first woman he could truly admit he liked. However, he would see her long enough to find out a weakness of The Last Riders then cut her loose like he did the rest of his women before she became entrenched in his life too deeply. He could fuck her and remain detached; he couldn't let her get too close because his life was too dangerous until he could talk Desmond into taking over completely. He didn't want to see her hurt; she had her own demons in her life to deal with without taking his.

He went back to work, stopping only when it became dark. He headed over to the shower in his adjoining bathroom and dressed in a clean suit for the night ahead.

Going downstairs, he sat in his booth, facing the door instead of the stage. When she came through the door, she was wearing a black leather miniskirt that barely covered her ass with heels that made her walk sexy as hell. Her top was a leather vest with tiny cutouts, and you could see her flesh underneath. Her black bra had a tiny amount of lace showing at the top. She slid into the booth across from him.

"What are you doing?" King asked.

She tilted her head at him inquisitively.

"Get your ass over here."

As Evie slid back out of the booth, King stood up, bending down to kiss her mouth. She opened to him immediately, letting his tongue in. When he found himself tempted to tongue fuck her, he broke away and guided her into the booth on his side before sliding in next to her.

"You're busy tonight."

"We're always busy."

"Is that Sherri on the stage?"

"Yes." Sherri was wearing a wig and mask tonight. She was always experimenting with costumes to see which would get her bigger tips.

"Ask if I can borrow that costume sometime. It looks like fun."

"No, it doesn't." She was dressed as a dominatrix.

"You're no fun. Don't you enjoy playing it kinky

sometimes?"

"Not when it involves me being the one flogged."

"Don't tell me, you can dish it out but can't take it."

"I've never used a flogger on a woman in my life."

"Want to?" Her question created images of her bent over his desk with her naked ass presented to him in the perfect position.

King laughed, shaking his head before he admitted, "I have laughed more in the last two days than I have over the last two years."

"You're too serious; you need to lighten up."

His private chef brought out two plates of food, setting them down on the table. Evie uncovered her plate, staring down at the burger and fries.

"Thank you, God. If I had to choke down one more pretentious meal, I was going to hit the nearest McDonalds on the way home."

"I could tell you weren't thrilled with last night's cuisine."

"Sorry, I'm just a plain woman with simple tastes."

"There's nothing plain about you, Evie."

She smiled up at him before digging into her plate of food, and they ate while Sherri danced. Evie watched the skills the woman used to entice the men. Hell, she was doing a pretty good job of enticing her.

"You into women, too?"

"No, but I can appreciate them. I like to snack, but when I eat dinner, I like a good steak."

"That's one way of putting it."

"Let me put it another way." Evie leaned into his side, running her hand along his thigh. She brushed his cock with her fingers before cupping it in the palm of her hand. "There are a couple of women at the club who like to get into pussy-eating contests. I'm not one of them."

A smile came to his mouth as he removed her hand from his groin. "I don't play in front of the staff."

"I knew you were boring." She leaned away from him.

"I need to check on the upstairs. Want to come?"

"Sure."

They went up the stairway into the crowded VIP room. King saw her to a booth before checking on a few things in his office. When he came back out, Evie was bent over Juliet, licking the remains of a body shot from the woman's stomach.

King felt his cock harden behind his pants. Going to the bar, he took a drink of whisky that Garth, his bartender, had waiting for him.

"Can I get an introduction when you're finished with her?"

"No." He took out his phone, calling security and giving an order.

He watched from the bar as Evie finished her body shot, helping Juliet to her feet afterward at the same time he saw the two couples coming angrily out of the private sex rooms. He motioned for one of the girls responsible for cleaning the rooms, advising her of what he wanted.

He then went back to watching Evie as she talked with Juliet, handing her the money for the body shot. When he saw the cleaner come out, he went to Evie, wrapping an arm around her waist then leading her to the prepared room.

"Where are we going?" Evie asked.

He led her into the bedroom, locking the door behind them. He tapped on the two-way mirror. "Take a break."

Confident his order would be followed, he turned back to Evie. "That was sexy as fuck; you have me hard as a rock."

"Let me take care of that problem for you." She gave him a wicked grin before reaching down to take off her skirt.

"Leave it alone; I want to fuck you with it on."

"You like the skirt?" Her hands smoothed the leather down over her hips.

"I fucking love the skirt," he said, moving forward as

she backed up teasingly toward the bed.

"You should see the one I have in red."

"You can wear it for me tomorrow night."

"I might not want to come see you tomorrow night." She sat down on the edge of the bed, and King came to a stop before her.

"Then I need to make sure you have fun tonight, don't I?"

Chapter Twelve

Evie licked her bottom lip, already planning on giving him a blowjob to take the edge off. Instead, she found her legs swept out from underneath her as her ass rode the end of the bed. King went to his knees, placing her thighs over his shoulders.

"Jesus, no underwear?"

"I didn't want to waste time." His cock swelled even harder at her words.

The woman enjoyed sex without any embarrassment. There was no wondering if he was going to get laid when it came to her. Once she had given herself to him last night, she had turned her body over to him to use any time. The women he had fucked before, he had felt as if he had to offer a bribe to keep their thighs open; expensive dinners, jewelry or luxurious surroundings. However, Evie only wanted his cock and the pleasure he could give her.

He leaned forward, sliding his tongue through her slick pussy. "Are you wet for me or Juliet?"

"Take your pick; you're both hot," she teased.

"I never felt like I was competing with one of my shot girls before."

He slid his tongue inside her pussy, fucking it with his tongue. When he felt her breathing accelerate, he pulled back.

"Don't stop; I was about to come."

"Get on the bed." King took off his shoes and opened his pants. Unbuttoning his shirt, he got on the bed next to Evie, taking her mouth in an erotic kiss before flipping her on her stomach and guiding her to her knees. Taking out a condom from his back pocket, he put it on then put his cock at her opening.

Evie's moan nearly had him coming before he could give her his cock. She whimpered as he thrust his length into her.

"You need my cock, baby?"

"Yes... harder, King. I need it harder." Evie thrust her ass back at him, trying to fill her needy cunt, but the bastard only let her have an inch at a time. Her frustration built at his incredibly slow movements.

"Please..."

"I don't like to share. The next time you want to play with a woman, I'll pick her. Understand me?"

"O...okay."

At her agreement, he let her have a little more.

"Dammit, King. Fuck me!" she screamed in frustration.

"I'm not ready for you to come."

He lifted her skirt so her ass was bare then pulled down sharply on her top until her breasts popped out of her bra, her low-cut leather top cupping them and pushing them up. His fingers found a hard nipple, pinching it tightly between his fingers. When Evie started shaking, her ass quivering, his hand went to her hair, winding it around his hand before pulling her head back while he rode her pussy.

"You bored?"

"God, no."

"I didn't think so," he said, thrusting into her with harder strokes.

Evie thrust back against him, desperately trying to

come. Broken whimpers passed her lips; she was hung on a precipice, unable to fall. Suddenly, she felt a movement behind her then the snap of his belt across her ass.

"Yes, harder," Evie begged him.

"Which one? My dick or the belt?"

"Both."

Evie screamed when she felt the belt against her ass again. He switched to her other ass cheek, giving it a hard hit. She came with her ass on fire, begging for more as her climax rolled into another one. King groaned, gripping her nipple harder as he also came.

When they were finally able to catch their breaths, they fixed their clothes.

"You okay?" King asked, studying her bottom before she tugged her skirt down.

"Hell, yes, I'll remember this every time I sit down for the next couple of days."

"Woman, you're making me hard again, and we have to give the room up. The rooms were booked for the rest of the night and now we're behind an hour."

"We could have waited until we got back to your place."

"Not after I saw you lick Juliet."

"Wait until you see her give me a lap dance." Evie could immediately tell the image was playing havoc with his dick.

Ushering her out of the room before she could tempt him to fuck her again, they settled back into his booth. She watched the show while he answered his employees' questions and watched the dancers.

Evie saw the crowd had increased since they had been upstairs, recognizing a few faces in the room. She noticed them glance several times at the table.

"Do the Predators come here often?"

"Yes. I have the best show in town."

Somehow, Evie didn't think it was just the show that brought them in. Evie looked the men over carefully. They rivaled The Last Riders in testosterone; she was glad the two groups didn't live near each other. While they had made peace with them after Eightball had been kidnapped and Penni had been taken in retribution, it wouldn't take much to set the men off in a clash.

"I need to take a call in my office. I'll be right back. Try to stay out of trouble."

Evie gave him an innocent look, which had him narrowing his eyes in warning. Yet, as soon as she saw the door close behind him, she went to greet the Predators.

"Hi, Ice," Evie said, stopping at his table. The voluptuous blonde, who had taken up residence on his lap, glared at her.

When he didn't immediately respond to her greeting, the group of men went silent as they listened to the interchange between her and their President.

"Do I know you?"

"I'm Evie. I saw you the night you helped out Lily in Treepoint. Then in the diner before you left town."

"You belong to The Last Riders?"

"I do."

"Then why you over here bugging me?" These assholes weren't the friendliest bikers she had ever met, but she didn't let their attitude faze her.

Her eyes flickered over their faces, memorizing them before her gaze was caught and held by the one at the back of the room sitting in the shadowy corner. His face was fucked up, giving him a menacing appearance.

"Everything okay?" King's voice came from behind her.

She looked over her shoulder at him. "I was just saying hi. I remembered them from Treepoint. Especially that one; he must be the one who took Penni for a long ride," she said as she pointed to Jackal in the corner.

"She miss me?"

Evie tensed, getting to the real reason she wanted to talk to the bikers. "Aww, that's cute. I'm glad you can make a joke about it. I want to pass along a little friendly warning: Fuck with her again and your little boy band will be squashed into a tiny, little enema, which I will personally shove up your ass."

Every man at the table stiffened. "Are The Last Riders threatening us?" Ice's astounded expression glared at her.

"Fuck no. I'm threatening you. Do not touch her again."

"That's enough, Evie. I think they got the message."

"I hope so, because I taught her how to use that gun she brought back. Personally, I think she should shove it up that motherfucker's ass herself."

King hastily turned her around, giving her a small push in the direction of his booth. "Go sit down."

Evie sashayed her ass back to his booth, stopping at the bar to nab herself a whiskey, telling the bartender to give her his most expensive brand. Taking her glass, she sat back down and waited for King to return while she watched the men interact.

She had deliberately pissed them off; several of them were still glaring at her. She lifted her glass in their direction before taking a drink then watched King calm them down, her question answered. The King of Queen City controlled the Predators.

King came back to the table. "Henry's waiting for you outside."

She smothered down her hurt feelings, sliding out of the booth then reaching down to pick up her purse. She walked toward the front door, not letting their gloating looks get to her. Outside, they took a step toward his car.

"Don't pull that shit again, Evie. Those aren't people you can fuck with."

"Neither am I." She slid into the backseat of the car, not flinching when he slammed the door shut.

Chapter Thirteen

"You're up early," Penni said when she came out of the bedroom.

Evie was wearing one of Train's t-shirts and her house slippers. Going to the kitchen, she poured herself a cup of coffee, taking a drink before she answered. "I don't need much sleep," she lied without remorse. She'd had a terrible night; the dark shadows under her eyes looked purple.

"Any plans today?" Penni chirped.

Evie stared at her balefully. "I have some research I need to take care of today. What are you up to?"

"I have to go out of town for two days, looking at the venue for a Mouth2Mouth concert. It's under renovation, so I want to make sure it's on schedule to be completed in time for their concert or we're going to cancel."

"Going alone?"

"Yes."

"Girl, you need to get a life."

"I will. I have a plan. I'm going to focus on my career for the next two years, meet someone, date for three years, then get married."

"I need another cup of coffee," Evie proclaimed. "I

hope you scheduled an orgasm in there somewhere."

"As soon as I see a man capable of giving me one, I'll let you know."

"You're surrounded by rockers," Evie said helpfully.

"Too much competition. You should see how many women chase after them."

"I'll pass."

"I have a date next week."

"Who with?" Evie asked, topping off her coffee; Shade's sister was too freaking perky first thing in the morning.

"Lily's old boyfriend, Charles."

Evie burned her tongue on her coffee at the same time she accidently spilt it. Turning away from Penni, she grabbed a paper towel to clean up her mess. "When did this happen?"

"Lily gave me his number when she found out we were having a concert there."

"Really?"

"Yeah. He's a nice guy, according to Lily. Goes to church and everything."

"He sounds like a prince. When's your date?"

"Next Saturday. I'm meeting him after the concert. We're going out to eat, and he's going to take me back to my hotel afterward."

"Sounds like he's got it all planned out."

"I know. It's really convenient."

"That's what I'm thinking."

Penni looked at the clock on the kitchen wall. "I have to go or I'm going to be late. See you later."

"Call me when you get off your plane."

"Yes, Evie. Jeez, you sound like my mom."

A knife of pain shredded Evie's heart.

"Evie…?" She gave her a smile.

"You better go. You'll miss your flight."

"You sure?"

"Go, girl, have some fun. Get laid, but be safe," she

added sternly.

"I'll try." Penni laughed, her natural exuberance coming back.

Evie waited until the door closed before picking up her phone on the counter, hitting Shade's call button.

"What's up?"

"Guess who your sister has a date with next Saturday?"

"Who?"

"Lily's ex, Charles."

The phone disconnected.

"He could at least have thanked me," she said to herself, carrying her cup to the computer desk.

Opening her computer, she began her search. Several clicks later, she had a list of names ready. Picking up her phone, she made some calls to a few old friends in the military then stood up. She was about to get another cup of coffee when she heard the intercom buzz. Walking over to the wall, she hit the button.

"Yes?"

"King is here to see you. Should I let him come up?"

"No."

"Do you have a message for him?"

"Tell him to fuck off. You can pass that along verbatim if you want to." She hung up the phone, reminding herself to tip him the next time she saw him downstairs.

She had poured herself another cup of coffee, pulling the chair to sit down again when a knock came at the door.

"Evie, let me in."

Evie closed the computer's windows, going to another screen to erase her browser. She then shut the computer before going to answer the impatient knocking.

"What do you want?"

King came in through the door as soon as she opened it, casting her an angry look. "Why didn't you let me up?"

"Because I didn't want to see you," Evie snapped.

"Why?"

The man couldn't be that stupid, could he? "Because

you dumped me in your car last night and sent me home."

"I was mad as hell. You challenged a dangerous group of men."

"Well, I'm mad now, so we're even." Evie put her hands on her hips.

"Whose t-shirt is that?"

"What?" She was briefly confused by the change of subject.

"Whose fucking t-shirt are you wearing?" King looked furious.

Evie licked her lips. "Train's."

"Take it off."

"You've got to be kidding me!"

"Take it off!"

When Evie jerked it off her head, throwing it at him, he caught it in midair. As soon as she threw it, she regretted it because of the look on his face.

"Don't you dare—" It was too late, the material was ripped and shredded within seconds. "I can't believe you just did that."

Evie launched herself at him, hitting whatever part of his body she could. However, she was quickly lifted and thrown over his shoulder as he turned toward the hallway. He walked down the hall, coming to a stop.

"Which one is yours?"

Evie didn't answer him, continuing to strike his back with her fists and kick out with her legs. He opened one door briefly before closing it and opening another, walking in and slamming the door shut with his foot.

He lowered her to the bed, following her down, then took her hands in one of his, pinning them down over her head. His lower body pressed her naked body to the bed.

"Evie, stop it."

Given no choice, she lay still, glaring up at him with furious eyes. "You had no right to do that, King."

"No, I didn't, but I did it anyway. I told you to take it off then you threw it in my face. Evie, since the day I met you, all I can think about is you with them, and it's driving me crazy."

She stiffened underneath him. "I don't want to hear anymore. Go, King."

"Why? Don't you want to hear the truth that I'm crazy for you, that I can't keep my mind on work? I haven't fucked a woman in one of those rooms since the first year I took over the club."

"King, this isn't going to work. I know you're just trying to use me to find out how to get to Shade, but I'm not going to let you use me against him. He saved my life, King. I won't betray him—ever." She quit trying to fight him, lying back against the bed. "Don't try to deny it, King. We know you had us checked out, and Shade knows exactly what and how much you know. You have to stop."

"I can't, Evie. She's my daughter." Evie felt the agony in his soul. He had screwed up with Lily, and as a father, he was trying to make it up to her.

"King, you're not going to change the past, however hard you try. I'm telling you, Shade loves her. Leave them alone. They deserve to be left alone."

As King lowered his head against her neck, shuddering, Evie's arms circled his shoulders, holding him close.

"I'll try." That was as good as she was going to get.

"Try hard," Evie responded, raising her head to brush his rough jaw with her mouth.

"I'll try," he repeated stubbornly.

Evie sighed, wrapping her legs around his waist. "Want to fuck?"

"What do you think?"

Chapter Fourteen

Evie's hand smoothed down the raincoat she had on. Leaning back in the seat of the cab, she looked out the window, barely holding her anticipation in check as the cab pulled over in front of King's apartment building. She pulled out the cash she had ready in her pocket, paying the driver before sliding out.

They had been spending a lot of time together during the four weeks she had been in Queen City.

She had been preparing this surprise for King for a couple of days now. Usually, they would spend the night together when he finished at the club. However, he had put his foot down about her coming to the club anymore, saying she was too distracting to him and the customers. He was going to be distracted tonight, for sure. She had borrowed one of Pepper's stripping costumes off her; the bright red outfit was garish and slutty. Evie was expecting a fun time tonight when she took off her coat, revealing her outfit.

He wasn't home yet, and she wanted to be waiting in the lobby when he came in.

The concierge gave her a strange look. "Good evening,

Evie."

"Hi, Anton. I'm just going to wait for King. I'll sit over there out of the way until he gets here." Evie started to go have a seat until she caught the look on his face. Her gut twisted.

"He's already here. Would you like me to give him a call and let him know you're here?"

"Is he alone?" Her throat went dry as she waited for his reply.

His silence was all the answer she needed.

She gave a brief smile. "Then there's no need to call. Thanks, anyway." She turned on her high heels, leaving the lobby to go back outside.

Evie stood there a moment before carefully crossing the busy street. Studying the buildings for several seconds, she found what she was looking for, wedging her body between two buildings. The shadows would hide her from anyone passing. She stood for over an hour on shoes that were beginning to pinch her feet.

Her usual time for arriving at his apartment was two a.m. At one thirty, Henry's car pulled up in front of the building. Her hands curled in the pockets of the coat as she let her weight shift to lean heavier into the shadows.

King came out, his arm circling the waist of a beautiful blonde. She appeared younger than her with a blue, ruched dress so tight Evie was amazed she could walk. King opened the car door for her and then bent down to give her a lingering kiss before helping her into the car. Shutting the door, he tapped on the roof, signaling Henry to drive away.

He didn't wait for his car to pull out before going back inside his building. Evie made herself relax her hands when she felt the sticky wetness of blood. She knew as soon as Henry dropped off the blonde, he would go to Penni's to get her.

She took her cell phone out of her pocket, calling a cab to pick her up. Thankfully, it was close by. As soon as it pulled up, she slid into the back seat. The driver gave her a startled look, which she ignored, giving him Penni's address.

As soon as the cab came to a stop, she got out and handed the driver the cash. Evie practically ran through the lobby to the elevator, controlling her rampaging emotions until she could get inside the apartment.

Penni turned around on the couch at her entrance. "Back so soon?"

"Change of plans. I decided to stay in; I wanted an early night. See you in the morning." Evie went into her bedroom before Penni could pose the prying questions Evie could see she was about to ask.

Inside her bedroom, she pulled off the coat, throwing it down on the floor and then kicking it away before taking off the red stripper outfit. She was so angry she wanted to tear it into pieces. Only the fact it didn't belong to her had her controlling her temper. Evie blinked back tears, not understanding why she was so upset.

Pulling on a t-shirt, she sat down on the end of her bed. She had fucked The Last Riders with the other women of the club, not giving a shit. Hell, she had been happy when they had begun getting married. Never once had she felt a pang of jealousy until she had seen King's mouth touch the blonde's.

When her cell phone vibrated next to her hip, she looked down to see it was a message from King. *Henry's waiting outside.*

Evie sat, staring down at the message.

Tired. Going to stay in. Goodnight. Evie pushed the send button.

Setting the phone down carefully on the nightstand instead of throwing it against the wall, she lay back on her bed and then turned off her bedside lamp. In her mind, she replayed King and the woman walking out of his apartment building. She wondered how many times over the last few weeks Henry had dropped off one of King's lovers just to pick her up afterward.

She curled into a ball. The most upsetting part was why she even gave a rat's ass. What had started out as a clear-cut mission of finding out if King's activities could in any way hurt Lily had developed into more. He had slid under her guard, seducing her into caring about him.

Evie remembered Beth's face when she had come to the hospital after being released, seeing Razer with Bliss. The pain of betrayal, both from Razer and herself as a friend for not standing beside her, had been something Evie had regretted for years. She had been loyal to the club and hadn't stood up for Beth, who had been terribly hurt. She wished she had Beth with her now.

Evie had always held part of herself back, keeping her past private. She needed Beth's quiet optimism to tell her everything would go back to normal. To convince her she really didn't care King had been fucking other women. The problem was, she did care.

Desperately, she clung to Levi's image. They had grown up together. He had been her first kiss, her first love. They had learned to ride bikes together, did Algebra together, went in the service together. He could fix a truck motor, install a kitchen counter and hunt, but at the same time, he could be as sweet and gentle as a spring breeze.

She hadn't been close to her parents or sister, always feeling on the outside. Levi had been her family, and when she had lost him, she had become a basket case.

When he had died, the woman she had been had also ceased to exist. She had survived her rape and losing Levi by becoming the antithesis of herself. She was no longer shy, timid or virginal; everything her sweet Levi had loved about her was gone, buried under years of parties, alcohol and men.

King had been resurrecting that woman, making her laugh again, making her care again. Well, he had shown her he could keep his emotions under control. She could, too. It was time she got back on track and did the job she had been sent to accomplish.

* * *

"What do you think?" King looked up from his phone at Desmond's question.

"About what?"

Desmond sighed, picking up his glass of wine. "About buying the McClure building. I think it will be a good return on our investment."

"Then buy it," King replied absently, placing his phone back in his suit pocket.

"What's going on? Why are you looking at your phone every five minutes?"

"No reason." King evaded his question, wanting to grind his teeth in frustration. Evie had been ignoring his calls and texts for three days. The man he had following her had said she had been all over his city, exploring and even hitting several of the bars. King couldn't understand the drastic change in her behavior. One night he was fucking her brains out, the next she wasn't giving him the time of day.

"You still seeing Evie?"

"I don't know," King answered caustically.

"What in the fuck does that mean?" Desmond asked, looking over his shoulder.

"It means she's not answering my calls," he snapped.

"Why don't you turn around and ask her?" Desmond nodded his head at a table behind them. "Of course, the man she's with might not appreciate it."

King frowned, turning around in his seat. Evie had her back to him; however, the man sitting at her table was in his early thirties with blond hair and a shit-eating grin aimed at Evie.

When King turned back around, Desmond was watching him with an amused expression. "Would you like me to go ask her for you?"

"I'm not in fucking middle school. I can do my own talking."

"Not if she's not returning your calls."

"Desmond, if you don't shut the hell up…"

Desmond laughed softly as their waitress approached with their bill. Signing the check, King and Desmond rose to their feet, avoiding Evie's table as they left the restaurant.

"I'll get in touch when the deal is finalized."

"Do that," King answered, waiting for Desmond's car to pull out before getting inside his own.

"Pull around to the side of the building," King ordered Henry.

King sat in the parking lot for twenty minutes before Evie and her date came out. She had her hair pulled up and was wearing a coral-colored dress. Her happy expression disappeared when she saw King leaning against his car with his arms folded across his chest.

"Evie, you haven't returned my calls." King's blunt words were loud in the quiet parking lot.

They came to a stop a few feet away.

"I didn't want to talk to you."

"Why not?" King glared at the man staring back and forth between Evie and him.

"Evie—" Her date began, but Evie quickly cut him off.

"Let's go, Kell." Evie took his arm, trying to sidestep King's car.

King glowered at him threateningly. "Do you know who I am?"

Kell nodded his head, his face going pale.

"Then get in your car and go," he ordered. "If I see you near her again, we'll be getting better acquainted. Do you understand me?"

His frightened eyes flashed to Henry who was sitting in the car.

"Wait just a fucking minute!" Evie said as her date high-tailed it to his car, not giving her a backward glance.

"Get in the car." King opened the rear door for her.

"Fuck off!" She spun on her heels, but before she

could take a step away, King had her, lifting her off her feet and tossing her into the backseat.

"Have you lost your mind?" Evie screamed at him, moving for the other door. King climbed into the car, shutting the door. Evie tried uselessly to get out of the car as Henry drove out of the parking lot. Giving up, she turned to him. "What do you think this is going to accomplish?"

"Are you going to tell me the reason you're no longer in my empty bed every night?"

She bristled at his words. "Empty? I doubt that. Why don't you call the blonde you were fucking the other night?"

A sinister smile crossed his mouth. "What blonde?"

"I don't fucking know her name. She was at your apartment the other night when I came early. I'll give you credit; you had it timed perfectly. One leaves, the other comes. Doesn't Henry get sick of chauffeuring your bitches around?"

"I don't know. I don't ask him. He gets paid to do what I tell him."

"Well, I'm not on your payroll. Take me to Penni's apartment," Evie commanded.

King moved closer to her on the seat. "You look beautiful tonight."

She gave him a dumbfounded look as he laid his hand on her thigh. "Are you high?" Her suspicious eyes searched his.

"No, I haven't touched drugs since I found out I conceived Lily when I was doing them. So, you haven't been talking to me because you're jealous?"

"I don't give a damn who you fuck." She denied his accusation.

"I think you do." His hand slid under the fabric of her dress which had ridden up to her knees when she had scooted across the car seat.

Her hand came down on his, trying to stop him

unsuccessfully.

"Why did you come by my apartment building early?"

"I was going to surprise you; I had borrowed an outfit from Pepper. Instead, I was the one surprised."

"Why? Did that bother you? You don't give a damn who The Last Riders fuck."

"I didn't care. I just wasn't in the mood for a threesome."

"I thought threesome's were your forte."

Evie's hand flew out, attempting to strike him, but King caught it, maneuvering her back against the seat until she was lying down with him between her thighs.

His hand went between her legs. "You're wet for me. Have you been missing my dick?"

Evie's hands curled as she attempted to claw at his face.

"Uh-uh, none of that." King jerked down her dress until her breasts popped out. Taking a nipple into his mouth, he began torturing the tip with his teeth. "I didn't fuck Lisa."

Evie turned her face away from him. "Don't lie to me," she whispered.

King bit down harder on her nipple before taking his mouth away. "I'm not lying."

"You've been seeing other women before I come to your apartment." Her accusing eyes stared up into his.

"Yes," he admitted. Evie tried to struggle from underneath him, but his mouth moved to her other breast. "Until I can walk away clean from Queen City, I won't jeopardize your safety. Those women are nothing but a smokescreen. They have a late dinner with me and a drink then leave."

Although Evie didn't believe him and her stiff body might be hiding the fact she wanted him, her wet pussy responded to the finger he thrust deep within. Her gasp turned to a moan as he began to slide his finger back and forth, moving his thumb to tease her clit.

Her hands grabbed his shoulders. "Henry will see.

Stop."

"The window is up. He can't hear and won't look." Brushing her objections aside, his mouth lowered to hers. "I haven't fucked another woman since you came to Queen City."

When she bit at his tongue as he tried to enter her mouth, King stopped rubbing her clit while continuing to finger-fuck her. She then opened her mouth, letting him have his way as his thumb returned to sliding through her wet pussy.

"Come home with me," he demanded.

"I don't need your protection."

"Evie, I'm not going to endanger you."

"Then get your hand away from my pussy!" she yelled at him, hitting at his shoulders.

King sat up in his seat, lifting off her.

"I'm too old to play these games, Evie."

"I'm not playing. If you really want to keep me safe, then all you have to do is stay the fuck away from me. Problem solved." As Evie folded her arms across her stomach, sitting tensely in her seat, King stared back at her. She was hurt, and while she was trying to hide it, it was unmistakable. Her eyes held the glimmer of tears, and the jackass that he was only then belatedly realized she was dressed like the sophisticated women he usually dated.

King pulled her onto his lap, his hand lifting her face to his. "You win, but we're going to play by my rules."

"Isn't that what we've been doing?"

"No more women acting as camouflage," King gave in. "And I better not catch you with another man again."

When Evie's mouth snapped open, he could tell she was going to lay into him.

"You won," he told her before she could yell at him. "The least you could do is accept it gracefully."

"I won? What did I win?" she asked snidely. "I want to go to Penni's apartment."

So, she wasn't going to forgive easily. King could deal

with her anger; what he couldn't work with was not seeing her.

King lowered the window long enough to tell Henry to take her home.

"Satisfied?" he asked with a lifted brow.

"No, I'm not." She crossed her legs.

King grinned at her unrepentantly.

"You're a jerk," she snapped, seeing his grin.

King shrugged, admitting his guilt.

It wasn't long before Henry pulled up in front of Penni's apartment. Coming to a stop, he got out to open the back door. Evie slid out, and once outside, she stopped and looked back inside the car.

"You coming?" she asked grumpily.

It wasn't the most seductive invitation he had ever received, but it was one that had his dick getting as hard as a brick in his pants.

Climbing out of the car, he ignored Henry's wink as he followed behind her.

"This doesn't mean I'm not still pissed." She pushed the button to retrieve the elevator.

"I understand." They walked into the elevator when the doors opened.

"If I find out you're lying to me about other women, I'll cut off your dick." She pushed the button to her floor.

King had to take a minute to keep from laughing at her vicious threat. "I won't."

The doors slid open and King followed behind her, watching the curve of her ass as she walked down the long hallway. She put the key in the door, but then turned back to him. "You better make it up to me for being such an ass in your car and leaving me hanging."

"Evie, if you would just open the door, I'll spend the night making everything up to you," he promised.

"In that case," Evie opened the door wide, "you better pace yourself; you have a lot to make up for."

"I think I can handle the job." King slammed the door

shut with his foot before sweeping her off her feet and into his arms, carrying her to the bedroom.

Two hours later, she was the one begging for mercy as she climaxed on his dick.

"Do you forgive me?" King asked as she stroked her damp hair back from her face.

"For what?"

Chapter Fifteen

As Evie drummed her fingertips on the table, King looked up from his paperwork amused.

"Bored?"

"I can only stare at Pepper shaking her tits for so long."

He had relented in letting her back in his club if she promised to behave herself. She had grudgingly agreed.

"Are you saying I need to get some new talent to keep you occupied?"

"Why don't you let Rory take the next set?" Evie cast him a hopeful glance.

"Because I don't want a riot on my hands. The men pay to see pussy, not dick."

To ease the disappointment in her eyes, he motioned for Henry to get one of his brands of expensive whiskey to pour her a glass. He had started having to keep his exclusive brands in his security room. Evie could drink like a fish, and she had developed a taste for his most costly labels. The bartenders had proven ineffective at keeping her to a limit when she would give them one of her seductive smiles.

Henry set her favorite down on the table. King poured

her a drink, watching her eyes light up in appreciation as she took a sip. It bought him enough time to finish the figures he was adding.

When she reached for the bottle, he forestalled her.

"One more."

King shook his head at her, stacking his papers together. "I have something better in mind."

"I doubt it." Evie's wistful look at the whiskey had him chuckling as he rose from the table, taking her hand.

"Come on, let's see if I can find something to keep you occupied."

He led her up the staircase to the VIP room, but instead of taking her inside, he walked down the hallway, coming to another door. Keying in his security code, he opened the door when the audible click sounded. King watched her reaction as she took in the elegantly furnished gaming room. He had spared no expense in setting up this room for the wealthy to spend a relaxing night pursing their pleasure.

Several pool tables were spaced evenly against one side of the room while card tables took the other half. A circular bar separated the two where a bartender and several of his bar girls kept the men plied with any drink they wanted. The bar girls weren't of the same caliber as the others in his club. No, these girls were exquisite, of exceptional beauty with bodies to match. It wasn't uncommon for them to leave after a night's work with several thousand dollars in their pockets, earned from serving the men drinks or on their backs in the rooms discreetly hidden at the end this one.

"Wow."

King smiled, pleased at her reaction.

"You've been holding out on me," she accused.

He took her to the bar, helping her slide onto one of the stools.

"I see this is where you keep Rory hidden." Evie nodded toward a back booth where the attractive man sat next to an older woman. She was clearly enraptured by the man, who oozed sex appeal.

"Evie, why is it I'm beginning to feel as jealous over Rory as The Last Riders?" His eyes narrowed on her.

Evie's unrepentant grin had his cock thickening. This woman was a handful. He had never met a woman who unashamedly enjoyed sex and made no pretenses about it. He found it refreshing and honest because he was usually surrounded with women who had become adept at feigning their responses. When Evie came on his cock, he knew she was experiencing a true orgasm, not play-acting to achieve whatever reward she desired.

"Can I play?" At first his temper began to soar, thinking she was talking about Rory, but then he realized she was now focused on a card game going on at one of the tables. Desmond, the mayor, and Tony Reid were playing.

"Afraid not. Choose another table. That's an Executive Game. It's by invitation only and the stakes are high."

"You don't think I can afford it?" Evie tilted her head to the side, studying his reaction.

"Can you?"

"Yes."

King hid his surprise. He was aware she was well set financially, but not to the extent she was insinuating. Then it dawned on him that The Last Riders must have given her the same financial stake they had given the original members, as she had been one of the first in the club. The patents The Last Riders held were worth a fortune. King had discovered the highly coveted patents when he had checked them out. He refused to acknowledge even to himself that it was a gesture that showed they were protective of her.

As if reading his mind, Evie gave him a wry smile. "The Last Riders have made sure that I can buy any purse I want. Money is not an issue for me. I also have an inheritance from my father's family. They were one of

Atlanta's wealthiest families. I grew up surrounded by old money and snobs. I can tell you the type of caviar by looking at it, and the year of a wine from the taste." Evie shuddered. "I've attended dinner parties for two different Presidents and traveled to countries most people only dream about."

King leaned against the bar. It was the first personal information she had revealed about her family.

"You're not close to your family now?"

"That's putting it mildly. My father and mother divorced right before I graduated high school."

"That must have been difficult," King surmised.

Evie shrugged. "I don't miss the parties or the people, and I sure as fuck don't miss the wine. I joined the service when I graduated and didn't look back."

"Wade, give me a tray of chips."

When the bartender set down a tray of chips on the bar, King slid them toward Evie.

"You want me to sign a note?" She looked at him questioningly.

"I think you're good for it." He touched the tray. "A hundred thousand enough?"

"To start with." Evie slid down from the stool.

King watched as she went to Desmond's table, asking to join. Desmond's eyes met his, and King gave an imperceptible nod. Consequently, Desmond got up from the table, pulling out a chair for Evie.

At first, the men dealt with her in a patronizing manner, thinking it was a joke until she won the first two games. King noticed a change come over the table as, one by one, they discerned they were dealing with a skilled player.

"They don't look too happy right now," Wade said.

"Give me a drink. I'm going to enjoy this." King settled on one of the stools as Evie meticulously and without mercy began to fleece his friends. The mayor lasted an hour before he threw in his hand, leaving with a frustrated expression.

"The girls aren't going to be happy," Wade commented as they watched the mayor leave without a backward glance.

The mayor would always pick one of the women to spend an hour with before he went home to his wife, often leaving a five thousand dollar chip for the banging session.

"He'll be back tomorrow night. He has to have his weekly fuck session to put up with his icicle of a wife."

The game continued with Evie winning. Desmond nor Reid were patronizing her any longer; both had a steely gaze that had King tensing on his stool.

Evie held her own throughout the night, winning and losing in equal turns with the men before she won the last game, pulling her chips to her and gracefully excusing herself from the game. Neither man looked pleased at her departure with their money, however.

He had watched her closely. She had played fair, and Desmond and Reid couldn't say otherwise. It must be a hard pill to swallow seeing her feminine ass walk away from the table with a large chunk of their money without having to blow them for it.

Evie came to stand next to him at the bar, sliding her original stake back to him.

"Wade, cash her out," King ordered.

Wade took her chips before going into the security room and coming back minutes later with a plain envelope of cash for her.

Evie opened the envelope and then pulled out a hundred and handed it to Wade.

"Can I buy you a drink?" Her seductive voice had King's hand curving around her waist, pulling her closer to his side.

"You can buy me the bottle."

Rory came to stand at the bar on the other side of Evie. "Two mojitos, Wade."

King watched as Evie turned at his employee's

masculine voice.

"She's only buying you a mojito? You're getting fucked before your clothes are off." King almost spit out his cigar at her remark. Rory, on the other hand, whose face held the seductively masculine look he had perfected, lowered his guard enough to actually smile at her.

"It's better than what I had to drink last night."

"What was that? Mai Tai." Evie winced, looking at him in pity.

King gritted his teeth, seeing Rory's customer begin to develop a frown. It wasn't a good look. The old bitch already looked like a hag.

"How much she giving you for tonight?"

"Evie." His sharp voice didn't stop Rory from answering.

"Ten thousand for the whole night."

"Take the night off." After Evie slid the envelope in her hand in front of him, Rory picked the envelope up, looking inside. He raised a brow at her.

"Are you sure you don't need any company tonight?"

I am seriously going to beat her when I get her back to my apartment, King thought.

"I already have my night taken care of, but thanks anyway. Maybe another night."

"I can't take your money without giving you something in return." Rory took a step forward, and before King could stop him, he swept Evie in a kiss that had King ready to punch him as Rory's client stormed from the room.

Rory lifted his head, breaking the passionate kiss. "If you change your mind, call me." He reached in his pocket and pulled out a card, handing it to her. King noticed Evie was slow in taking the card, still befuddled by the kiss.

"King?" Rory's eyes met his.

"Beat it. I'll call her and make it up to her." Although, both silently acknowledged it would be Rory kissing her ass to make amends.

"Thanks…?" Her breathy voice had King debating strangling her while everyone watched.

"Evie," King growled.

"Thanks, Evie. I'll see you around."

"Yes, you will." Evie leaned heavily against the bar as Rory left to enjoy his impromptu night off.

"King?" Evie sighed.

"What?" he snapped.

"You don't charge enough for him."

* * *

King stared down at Evie in the bed, the bedside lamp giving the room a muted glow. She lay sprawled out, naked on the mattress, her skin still bearing the imprint of his hand. He reached out, tracing the curve of her silky breast, noticing the gold chain around her neck.

His hand reached down, picking the thick locket up, fiddling with it and seeing a tiny button on the side. Pressing it with the tip of his nail, the top flipped back. A ring lay inside. King lifted it closer to see it better. It was a diamond ring. The diamond was small, but the ring probably cost a couple thousand. King wanted to rip the necklace from her then wake her up and fuck her again.

"It's not nice to snoop." Her soft recrimination had his eyes lifting to her drowsy ones.

"Who gave it to you?"

She lowered her eyelashes, her hand taking the necklace from him. "Levi, my high school sweetheart, gave it to me the day we graduated high school. He had saved his money up, working part-time for a year and a half." Her hand tightened on the ring.

"He was worried that the diamond would be too small. I told him I didn't even need a ring. I wanted to go to the court house and get married, but he talked me into waiting. He wanted to make sure he was what I wanted.

"He was afraid because we had grown up together that I couldn't be sure he was the one. His mother was our housekeeper. No matter how much I told him it didn't matter, though, he always felt the money between us."

"Was he right?"

King saw the hurt before she concealed it.

"Not about the money, about him being the one," King clarified his question.

"Oh." She took a moment, staring down at the ring. "No, I knew I loved him from then until the day he died. I still love him."

The answer to his question struck him inexplicably in the chest. Evie rolled over, lying on his chest. "I'm not an eighteen-year-old virgin anymore."

No, she wasn't. With her whiskey colored eyes and tumbled hair, she was a seductress. No shy virgin would be so confident as to press her nipples against his chest or slide her leg intimately between his thighs. A virgin wouldn't slide her hand down his stomach until she reached his cock, sliding her thumb over the crest.

When the tip of her tongue traced her bottom lip, his hand curled against the nape of her neck, tugging her down to him. His tongue invaded her mouth, taking control and enticing her by tracing the tender flesh behind her bottom lip before tangling their tongues together. She broke free, taking deep breaths.

"The list keeps growing. The Last Riders, Rory, and now Levi." King rolled until she was under him. Sliding between her thighs, he thrust his cock inside of her without any foreplay. "A man likes to know he's the only one in his woman's bed."

Evie's thighs gripped his hips while she put her hands in his hair, tugging him down to stare in his eyes.

"I am loyal to The Last Riders. I was teasing you with Rory. And Levi…" her voice broke, but she went on, "is not coming home. The eighteen-year-old Evie still loves him, but time doesn't freeze for anyone, and I'm not the same woman. I lost a part of her when those men raped me, another when Levi died, and the rest a piece each time I fucked someone."

King kept moving over her, imprinting his body on hers.

"If you want someone who's going to pretend you're her only one, then you're fucking the wrong woman,"

"I am not fucking the wrong woman." His hand tangled in her hair, driving his cock into her in hard strokes, dominating her body with his. "If you want to tell yourself that there is no part of that old Evie left, then go ahead, but I see her in you all the time."

Evie began to struggle against him as he took the necklace off, placing it on the bedside table. "You haven't worn this necklace since I met you. What's wrong? Am I getting too close?"

"No!"

"I think I am." King surged inside of her, driving past her defenses, making sure she was unable to hold her response back from him. Her fists quit hitting at him, circling his shoulders instead, her hips thrusting back against his. "You wanted to remind yourself that you belong to Levi. That's why you wore that ring to my bed. If you think I'm going to let you put a barrier between us, then you're fucking the wrong man."

"King!" Evie screamed as she came, sending him into his own climax.

King slid to her side, pulling the coverlet over her trembling body. A tear slipped out of the corner of her eye.

"I can't love someone like that again."

"Evie, I didn't want to love anyone, either, but the one thing I've learned in my line of work is, you can't stop a bullet once you've pulled the trigger."

Chapter Sixteen

Evie sat at the table in the back, looking for the man she was there to meet. He was always late; that was how he had gotten the nickname Rabbit when they were in the service. She was about to order another drink when she saw him come in the restaurant door.

His eyes looked around the popular restaurant until he saw her. As he drew closer to the table, Evie smiled in greeting.

"It's been a long time, Evie."

"Too long. You should come for a visit. I told you we would show you a good time."

"Jewell still there?"

"Of course."

"I'll pass," he said, shuddering.

Evie couldn't help but laugh. Jewell and Rabbit had, at one time, been a couple. They had broken up when Jewell had caught him in bed with another woman, though. She had refused to talk to or about him ever since.

"I don't know why you're holding a grudge; you're the one who fucked around."

They sat down at her table. "She nearly killed me.

Believe me, several states between us is for the best."

"How are you doing since you've been out?"

"Making a living."

"Doing better than that, from what I hear." In her search for information on King, she had discovered Rabbit had been gradually building his reputation as a middle man for transactions involving illegal commodities. He would make the buys and pay for what was wanted then deliver the goods to whoever had purchased his services. It was dangerous as shit, and she hoped he knew what he was doing. Some of the men he was dealing with made the hair on the back of her neck rise.

"You got what I need?"

Rabbit handed her a flash drive. "It's all there."

"Thanks. I put your money in the account number you gave me."

"I saw it before I came through the door." Rabbit had always been out for himself; that was why he and Jewell had never been good as a couple and he had ended up breaking her heart.

"Anything else I should know?"

"No. Everything else, I've already told you. King's been slowly turning control over to Ice, although Desmond Hart will be the one in charge as a silent partner. He's even transferring ownership of his strip club to Henry. He's getting out of the business as fast and clean as possible, and without ruffling any feathers."

That was the same information she had found out from two other sources. It was now obvious he was trying to keep Lily safe by giving up a business he had worked most of his life to build.

"He only has one little hiccup left and he'll be free."

Evie's hand froze in lifting her glass of iced tea. This was the first time she had heard this piece of news in the almost two months she had been in Queen City. It had taken her that long to dig through years of the filth he had fought his way out of to make sure there was nothing in his past or present to touch Lily. She had found, instead, that King was cleaning his own messes. She had been waiting for this report, ready to go back to Kentucky if it came back clean.

She ignored the ache at the thought of leaving King. She tried to tell herself it was just because she had shared his bed every night, not because she was developing feelings for him.

"What's the hiccup?" she asked, already dreading the answer from the look on Rabbit's face.

"There is a deal going down this weekend with Ramos. It's big."

"Is King buying or selling?"

"Neither. It's a shipment of black tar heroin. Ramos has a buyer, but the drugs accidently ended up in Queen City when the dumbass carrying it had to drop and hide it before he got arrested. Now Ramos has to come to town to sell it or take a loss, and Ramos doesn't like to lose money."

"Where does King come into this? No one sells drugs in Queen City without his approval and giving him a slice of the pie."

"Ramos doesn't give a fuck about doing either," Rabbit answered. "He's going to sell the drugs then leave without giving King his cut, which means the shit is going to hit the fan."

"What if King just ignores Ramos, lets him slide under his radar?"

"Ramos has been trying to branch out from New Mexico. He's testing the waters, so that wouldn't be a smart move."

"Dammit." This was not what she'd wanted to hear. "What's he going to do?"

"No idea. Maybe you should roll over and ask him tonight."

Evie ignored his smart-ass comment. "Who's buying the drugs?"

"A man named Morin."

"Where's he from?"

"No one knows. He's the wildcard. He's dealt with Ramos before, but that's all the information on him I could find."

Evie nodded her head, biting her lip.

"Anything else?" Rabbit started to stand.

"No, I think that will do it. If you hear anything else…?"

"You'll be the first to know. Bye, Evie."

"Bye, Rabbit."

Evie watched her old friend leave, sick to her stomach. King was *so* close; Evie hated that this one deal could wreck it all. She had to stay to make sure the deal went through without a hitch, and if not, that King didn't have a new enemy at the end of the day.

She paid her ticket then got up from her table and went outside. She then walked the three blocks back to Penni's apartment, making sure no one had followed her.

She waited until she was inside the apartment and was certain Penni wasn't home before she called Shade. He wasn't going to be happy with what she had learned. She was going to have to buy King some time to clean this mess up.

Shade answered the phone on the first ring.

"Can you talk?"

"Hang on." She heard him talking to Lily in the background before the sound of a door opening and closing came across the line. "Go ahead."

Evie explained everything she had learned. "He's getting out of the business, Shade."

"Then what's wrong?"

"There's a deal going down that could go bad. I have to see how it ends to know if he can walk away clean."

Silence came from the other end.

"Shade, he's not involved in the deal; someone's trying to piss on his doorstep."

"If he cared about Lily, he'd let them piss then hose the door down after they left."

"Give him a chance. He's trying."

"Evie..."

"Please, Shade?"

"What do you care?"

She didn't say anything for a minute. "I don't want to see Lily hurt, either, and losing her dad would hurt her, Shade." She had played the only card that would work to save King's life and that was Lily. If that didn't work, she was out of options.

"Let me know when the deal goes down and what happens. Do you need me to send a couple of brothers down as backup?"

"No, I'm good."

"Tell me the truth."

"I'm good, I swear. If there's any trouble, I'll call."

"Okay, you better. I won't be happy if you get hurt."

"I won't."

"Later."

"Bye, Shade." Evie disconnected the call, running her hand through her thick hair.

Going to the computer, she researched Ramos and Morin for two hours. When she was finished, she cleared the computer of all her searches.

She and King had started rotating apartments. They usually stayed at his penthouse, but when Penni was out of town with the band, she preferred to stay at her apartment. Both of them were more relaxed with their guards lowered on neutral ground.

Evie went to take a shower, dressing in jeans and a t-shirt. She wasn't going to the club tonight; he would have Henry come by to pick her up after it closed.

She had settled on the couch with a movie she had rented when Penni came in all smiles. "What are you doing tonight?"

"I was staying in until later tonight when King got off.

Why?"

"Because Vida, Sawyer and I are going clubbing tonight. Want to go?"

"Yes. Where are we going?"

"Flying Champion."

"I'll get changed." Evie started to go to her room.

"Evie? Can I borrow an outfit?" Evie stared at the blushing woman. "I don't have anything like… I mean…"

Evie held her door open. "Come into my room, the spider said to the fly," Evie joked. "I have just the outfit."

It took them over an hour to get dressed between trying on different clothes and doing their hair and make-up. When they were done, they stared at themselves in the mirror.

"Are you sure this is decent?"

"I never said it was decent. If you wanted that image, you sure as fuck shouldn't have asked to borrow *my* clothes." Evie was wearing her red leather skirt that was even shorter than her black one, which was on Penni. Both wore high heels, but Evie wore a black sequin top that flashed every time she moved while Penni wore a white leather halter top that left a V of flesh bare between her breasts. They had glued the material down so she didn't have to worry about her breasts popping out. Evie could just imagine men's horny gazes on the beautiful girl, hoping for a flash of tit they were never going to see.

Evie grabbed both their purses from their closets to swap them out. Dumping the contents of them into the smaller ones wasn't easy, though.

"Why do you carry so much shit around with you?"

"I forget to clean it out." The girl shrugged. Evie counted five fingernail files, six polishes, three checkbooks, four packs of gum, and two granola bars.

"You could live out of that purse." Shoving Penni's wallet and keys into the smaller purse, she was about to close it when she hesitated and opened her own again, taking out a small package and placing it in the one she was lending to Penni.

"Was that a condom?"

"You never know when you need to be prepared."

Penni burst out laughing, stopping suddenly when Evie tossed her work purse to the side. "Be careful." As the gun Shade had let her have slid out, Evie barely caught it in time.

"Penni, you were supposed to keep it close in the apartment, not pack it around with you everywhere."

"It makes me feel safer."

"*It doesn't* me. You would have to dumpster dive to find it in that purse of yours. I'll put it over here for now." Evie placed it under the couch cushions.

Penni looked down at her phone. "Vida and Sawyer are downstairs. Ready?"

"Let's go have some fun."

Chapter Seventeen

King picked up his ringing phone. "Yes."

"She's at the Flying Champion with Vida, Sawyer, and Penni," Lou informed him. He was one of his best men, handpicked to keep an eye on Evie while she was in town.

"She's having a busy day." Lou had also called him earlier that day to tell him of her meeting with Rabbit before she went back to the apartment she shared with Penni.

"They're drawing attention."

"What kind of attention?" When his phone pinged, he took the phone from his ear, touching the screen. He gritted his teeth when he saw how Evie was dressed. His hand clenched around the phone when he put it back to his ear. "If anyone touches her, you're fired."

"How in the fuck am I going to do that? You told me not to let her see me."

"I'm on my way." He motioned to Henry to get the car. She had texted him two hours ago, saying she wouldn't be able to see him tonight. However, he had thought she had a headache or wasn't feeling well.

"Going somewhere?"

King hadn't noticed Jackal coming down the steps from the VIP room until he spoke to him. Jackal had used him to book an hour of Juliet's time. Hell, the woman had been begging to give it to him for free for the last six months. Instead, Jackal had paid for his pleasure so the woman wouldn't get any ideas that there was anything more to it than just sex.

"Seems my girl wants to play in someone else's playground tonight." King flung his phone down angrily while he gathered his papers.

Jackal reached out, snagging his phone before King could stop him. He stood staring down at the phone, stone-faced. Lou had snapped the picture while Evie and Penni had been dancing, and both women were dressed to get laid. King crushed his cigar between his teeth, thinking about the picture.

"They're at the Flying Champion?" Damn, he was good to figure that out from the picture.

"Yes, it seems they went out with Vida and Sawyer, too. Where in the fuck are Kaden and Colton tonight? Can't they keep better control of their wives than that?"

Jackal didn't reply, setting King's phone down on the table then taking his own phone out of his leather jacket. "Brother, where are you?"

King got up from the table.

"You cool with your wife partying at the Flying Champion?" Jackal moved the phone away from his ear, disconnecting the call. An evil smile came to his twisted lips. "They didn't know. I wonder which is the most pissed."

King picked up his paperwork. "Me."

* * *

Evie raised her arms in the air, thrusting out her hips, jumping up and down to the beating music.

Penni repeated her moves across from her as the beat escalated in the song. They grinned at each other as they danced, having a good time. Evie couldn't remember being so carefree, trying to think of the last time. Probably since she was younger than Penni, just graduating high school.

When Sawyer and Vida joined them on the dance floor, the women tried to out-maneuver each other to see who could dance the most seductively. Evie gave up when she saw Vida's moves; the former stripper had them all beat with her natural sultriness Yet, Penni gave her competition, also. What the girl lacked in skill, she made up for in enthusiasm.

Evie tossed her hair, her eye catching a grim face watching them.

"Shit!"

"What?" Penni asked.

"King's here."

"Who cares?" Sawyer said, wiggling her hips and thrusting her ass out. "We're modern women; we're allowed to have fun without men telling us what to do."

"I'm glad you feel that way, because Kaden and Colton are here, too."

Vida almost tripped, and Sawyer's ass quit shaking to the beat.

"Where are they?" Vida asked.

"Waiting for us at the table."

"I'm going out the back door," Sawyer moaned.

"What happened to *I am woman, hear me roar*?" Evie asked sarcastically over the loud music.

"It went out the door when I saw Kaden's face. Vida and I told them we were going out to dinner, not clubbing."

Penni laughed at the women as they stood frozen, no longer dancing. Her eyes were on a good-looking man leaning against the bar, giving him 'come hither' looks.

Penni piped up, "It can't be that bad. What can they do?" The three women stared back at the innocent woman which brought another laugh from Penni.

"Hold me back," Evie told Vida.

"Okay, I'll stop. But seriously, you three should see

your faces. What do you want to do?"

"What can we do?" The three women filed off the dance floor, heading back to their table. Penni peeled away, going to the bar and flirting shamelessly with the man she had been ogling.

"Traitor!" Sawyer seethed.

Evie made sure she was the last in line coming to the table, deciding to brazen it out when she saw his coldly-furious face.

"King!" She wrapped her arms around his shoulders, pressing her breasts against his chest.

"What are you doing here?"

"Penni begged us to come out with her. She said she would go alone if we didn't, so we came out to make sure she was safe," Evie flung Penni under the bus without qualms. She also noticed Vida and Sawyer both nodded at her explanation.

"This is a meat market." King's steady gaze didn't move from her face.

"I know! That's what we told her. You know how innocent she is; we were protecting her."

Penni's seductive laughter could be heard over the crowd.

"Is that her practically forcing her tongue down that man's throat?" King's sarcastic question showed he wasn't impressed with her explanation.

Evie was going to kill Penni.

"She's had too much to drink. I need to go get her." Evie turned on her heels; she was going to slap the girl silly when she got her hands on her.

"That won't be necessary." King reached out, grabbing the waist of her skirt and holding her in place.

"Why not? I promised Shade to—" The sentence died abruptly as she noticed several large men were cutting a swathe through the crowded nightclub. Evie swallowed hard. Fuck. The Predators had invaded the nightclub and were heading for the bar. Unsuspecting, Penni had her back to them while she kissed the man who had placed his hand on her ass, pulling her to him.

Evie watched, fascinated as the bikers surrounded them. She couldn't see what was going on with her friend surrounded by the large bikers, and she didn't like that one bit. "Why are they here?"

"They must be protecting Penni."

"She needs protection *from* them."

A second later, the crowd parted so Evie could see Penni arguing with the one who had a scar on his face. He made a comment, and Evie could see from Penni's face it was bad.

"Uh, oh," Evie said when she saw Penni starting to hit him with her purse.

"Why is she hitting Jackal with her purse?" King asked her.

"She has a little bit of a temper," Evie answered.

Penni continued to hit the biker who raised his arm to protect himself while jerking her purse out of her hand. The purse, which only had a simple snap closure, immediately flew open, spilling the contents of the purse onto the floor.

As Penni dropped to the floor, picking up the scattered contents and putting them back in her purse, her face blushed bright red when Jackal took the foil packet out of her hand. Penni got back to her feet, jerking it out of Jackal's hand before putting it back in her purse.

"You ready?" King picked up her purse from the table.

"What? I can't leave Penni when—"

"Ice is going to make sure she gets home safely for me." As King maneuvered her through the crowd, she looked back at Vida and Sawyer, who both seemed to have their hands full of angry husbands.

"King, you're overreacting."

King didn't say anything, leading her through the doorway to his car. Henry watched their approach with a grin.

She slid in the car, turning back to King who slid in after her. Her mouth snapped open, ready to give him hell then closed it just as quickly when she saw the expression on his face he was no longer attempting to hide. Her instincts had her scooting away from him, hugging the opposite door as Henry closed his.

King leaned back indolently against the expensive leather, smoothing out his pants with an elegant hand. "Why didn't you tell me where you were going?"

"I don't have to tell you what I do every minute of the day."

"No, only when you meet middle men and fuck around on me."

Damn.

Evie gathered her temper. "First off, I resent your lack of trust. Secondly, I served in the military with Rabbit. I heard he was in town, and we met for lunch. That was it. Penni wanted to go out; I went with her. I had no intention of fucking around tonight."

King picked up her purse that was lying on the seat between them. Opening it, his hand reached inside, pulling out the condoms. "Then why did you need these?" He put them back in her purse, closing it then handing it to her.

"I don't owe you any explanations," Evie said, looking out the window.

"Yes, you do."

After the car had pulled up in front of King's building, Henry opened the door for them. They walked through the lobby in silence. The ride in the elevator was filled with tension.

Inside the penthouse, King went to the bar, pouring them both drinks while Evie stood stiffly by the couch, shivering at King's cold attitude. She had never seen this side of him. She had seen his arrogant and stubborn side, and she had seen him run his club with a business attitude, always maintaining a professional *façade*. But not this cold, detached side.

The man standing across the room from her, unbuttoning his shirt to show his muscular chest, was a man who had fought his way up from the streets, willing to do whatever it took to take what he wanted.

"I think this is partly my fault; I did not make myself clear. I expect a certain type of behavior from my woman, and one of those is not to fuck other men when she's mine."

"I'm not yours."

"Yes, you are. You don't want to admit it, but you are, Evie. All mine."

When Evie shook her head, King set his glass down on the bar. She expected him to grab her, so she tensed, preparing to fight him. Instead, he went to the window.

"Come here." Evie dropped her purse on the counter, moving to stand at the window, staring out like he was.

"That is my city. I own every person in it. Most don't know it, but I do. Just like you."

Again, Evie started to shake her head, yet in the next instant, he had moved so fast she didn't have time to react. He jerked her top and bra from her body then ripped her skirt away. Evie trembled as she stood naked in front of him, only wearing a black thong that barely covered her shaved pussy.

He pressed her back against the window. "You put this tat on you, showing you belong to The Last Riders, but I'm going to pay Colton for a cover-up. My name will cover it because you belong to me now."

Her hands went to his shoulders to push him away. "I belong to *them.*"

"Exactly who do you belong to? Train? He fucks anything that moves. Rider? He likes sharing, doesn't he? But he doesn't want to claim anyone. Cash? Hell, he won't even let you sleep in his bed. Viper? He belongs to Winter. Knox? He belongs to Diamond. Shade? He belongs to Lily. I can keep on going, Evie. You're just a fuck-toy to those men."

"Shut up," Evie screamed.

"What's wrong, Evie? Does the truth hurt?"

"No. It doesn't. I don't belong to them; I'm a part of them. They have my back. They protect me."

"They use you."

"No, they don't. It's the other way around." Evie laughed at his shocked expression from her admission. "They give me support for…"

"For what?

"For everything," Evie went on, ignoring his questioning gaze. "They give me what I need when I need it. Train and Rider can both fuck me until I'm too tired to think and can sleep. Cash can take control away when I step out of line. Viper, he helps me make important decisions. They gave me shares of their business. I'm a very wealthy woman because of them. Knox, he's my best friend. He understands what it's like not having the one you love."

"What does Shade give you?"

"None of your fucking business!"

"Has he fucked you since he's been with Lily? Has he already betrayed her?"

"I've never fucked Shade! He saved my life. He was the one who found me after those men raped me. He cleaned me up and stood beside me when everyone else called me a whore. He let me stay at his house with his mother and Penni when I got out of the service. He made sure I got counseling. When I joined The Last Riders, he tried to talk me out of it. He never gave me his vote, but I needed The Last Riders, and he finally backed down. He gave me someone I could talk to, and I was someone that could listen to him talk about Lily. That's how I know he will never hurt her; he's done nothing but talk about her for years."

"Why didn't you tell me?" King's shoulders slumped with defeat. Evie knew he only wanted to hear bad things about Shade, not that he was in love with his wife and had longed for her for years.

"Because it's none of your fucking business!"

"Anything to do with you or Lily concerns me. When are you going to understand? You're not a fuck-toy to me, Evie. I care about you." His hand cupped her cheek.

"You don't care about me, King." Evie contradicted him.

"You're wrong. It's too late." He turned her to face the window, pressing against her back. "You're mine like every building, man and woman out there belongs to me. I'm never going to let you go."

Chapter Eighteen

"King, I can't stay here."

His mouth traced a line from one bare shoulder to the other. "Why not? They have so many women they won't even miss you."

"That's not true." She couldn't keep the hurt out of her voice.

"Tell me one who would miss you? Which one would it cause to eat their heart out if you didn't wake next to them? Who would miss you bad enough to come after you? No one. You've been gone for the last two months. How many times have they called you? Told you to hurry back?"

"Stop it, King." He didn't know what he was talking about. It had been several days since they had last called, but they were all busy. It was the factory's busiest time.

"I can't spend an hour in which I don't want to know where you are, what you're doing. I fuck you hard so you're tired enough to sleep, wake in the middle of the night to make sure you still are, and when I wake in the morning, it makes my day to hear your grumpy voice before I walk out the door. If you left, I would not only miss you, I would come after you and bring your ass back here where you belong—with me." His hand went to her hair, tilting her head back while keeping her body pressed to the window.

She heard him unzip his pants, and Evie trembled at the erotic touch of his hand as his fingers slid under her thong, sweeping through her damp pussy and coming to a stop when he reached her clit. He stroked the hood until she pushed her ass back against him, wanting more.

Placing her hands on the window in front of her, she braced herself when she felt his cock brush against her opening before sliding inside her in a movement so hard her breasts were pressed flat against the window. Her legs widened to ease his entry.

"King…"

His hand tightened, bringing her head back to rest on his shoulder as he began fucking her, staring down into her eyes. The violet depths of his eyes swirled with emotions his image branded her soul. She rose onto her toes in the high heels, trying to give herself more of him.

"What are you going to do, Evie? Does being mine scare you so badly?"

"Yes," Evie admitted out loud to both of them. "You're using me. You want to hurt them."

"Not if it means hurting you. Believe me, Evie; why would I lie? I have nothing to gain except you, and that's all I want."

Evie shuddered as he continued to fuck her, leading her desire where he wanted it to go, taking the control away from her but giving her what she needed in return.

She moaned as his finger rubbed her clit hard while he drove inside of her harder. She couldn't tear her eyes away from him anymore than she was beginning to believe she would be able to leave him.

Her pussy began rippling in the beginning of her climax, and it was then she realized he hadn't worn a condom. She had broken a rule of the club; she had fucked without a condom. She closed her eyes tightly as she felt both of them climax, stealing away her last chance of escape.

Somehow, someway, King had managed to steal his way into her heart, so she was going to take a chance and trust him. She had to at least give them a chance; she wanted that happily ever after just once for herself.

King stepped back from the window.

"It's a good thing I'm not afraid of heights," Evie joked, trying to make light of the connection she felt between them.

"I would never let you fall. I'll always be there to catch you." He picked her up, carrying her through the bedroom and into the bathroom. He slid off her high heels like she was Cinderella then lifted her into the shower, turning the water on. They washed off in silence.

When King turned the water off, he pulled her from the shower. Evie then stood at the mirror while he brushed and blow-dried her hair. He treated her as if she was special, as if she meant something to him.

When he was finished, she turned back, taking his hand then leading him to his bed where she pushed him down onto it. "Don't think I didn't notice you didn't use a condom."

King's hand reached out to play with a nipple. "I got carried away."

"You don't get carried away."

"You on the pill?"

"No, implant." Evie bent over his chest, laying her head down so she could hear his heartbeat.

"What are you doing?" She heard his rumbling laughter.

"Making sure you have a heart."

"I have one." He took her hand, placing it on his chest, his gunshot wound just a few inches higher.

Her head dropped to his chest again. "I don't know how to love you, King, but I'm going to try." She let her heart shine in her eyes for a brief glimpse, begging him silently not to hurt her, giving him her trust.

"Evie…" King's voice softened. Neither one of them was used to exposing their hearts. Both of them were used to guarding them while wanting to reach out and take their own grasp at happiness.

Evie did something then she hadn't allowed someone to do in years. He pulled her close, hugging her tight, while she wrapped her own arms around him, hugging him back just as tightly.

* * *

Evie woke when the first rays of sunlight started to rise from the sky. Sliding quietly out of bed, trying not to wake King, she went into the bathroom.

Remembering her phone, she went into the other room to get it; she wanted to make sure Penni hadn't left her any messages after their fiasco of clubbing.

She crossed the room, picking up her skirt and top from the floor before going to the couch where she picked up her purse, accidently knocking down the folder King had packed into the apartment with them.

She wasn't going to read them; she had found out everything she already needed to know. She slid the papers back into the folder, rising to her feet, and she was about to set them down when King startled her.

"What are you doing?"

Evie smiled at him tenderly.

"You couldn't even do it one day, could you?"

"What?" Evie asked, confused as to why he was becoming angry.

King motioned to the folder she still had in her hand. "Snooping again? By now you should know I don't keep anything for you to find in the apartment. Didn't Rabbit tell you yesterday I was getting out of the business?"

"You've been watching me? That's how you knew I was at the nightclub last night?"

"Of course, why would I trust you?" King snapped.

Evie felt as if a hole had been drilled in her heart. Setting the file down, she began getting dressed, giving herself time to get her emotions back under control. She finished putting them on then walked across the room to him. Without saying a word, she went into the bathroom, picking up her thong and throwing it into the trashcan, then putting on her heels.

"What are you doing?" Ignoring him, she slid by, walking back through his bedroom. He grabbed her arm in the hallway.

"Let me go." Her deadly-calm voice had him dropping her arm.

Evie went to the couch, picking her purse back up. "Get yourself out of the mess with Ramos. I don't care how, just do it. I checked them out. Ramos plays dirty. He's the type to try to use Lily against you. Let him do his deal or let the Predators deal with it. Either way, go back to Treepoint and visit Lily until the deal's over." Evie went to the door, opening it and closing it behind her.

Once in the elevator, she shut down every emotion she had, shoring the barricades she had let crumble last night. She had known better; she couldn't believe she had fallen for his lies. He had told her he wouldn't let her fall, yet she felt as if she was in a downward spiral she wouldn't be able to recover from.

Going out into the daylight, she started walking down the city street toward Penni's apartment when she heard a car come up behind her. She didn't have to turn to know who it was.

Henry pulled up, rolling the window down. "Get in, Evie."

"Go away, Henry. Please, just leave me alone."

The man nodded and the electric window slid back up. Evie continued walking, her feet becoming sore and tired, but she refused to ride in his car or have anything to do with King again.

The car followed her until she stumbled into Penni's

apartment building.

Penni was sitting at the table, jumping up when she saw her. "What happened?"

"Nothing. I'm fine. Make sure you lock the door when you leave for work and inform the concierge that if someone comes knocking on the door without permission, I'll call the owner and complain about him not doing his fucking job."

"Okay, do you need me to get you something?"

"No. I'm going to lie down for a while. I'll see you tonight." Evie shut her bedroom door before Penni could pry any further.

Limping into the bathroom, she started to run water into the tub before getting undressed and climbing inside, hissing in pain as her blistered heels were engulfed in the warm water.

Evie drew her knees to her chest, wrapping her arms around her legs. She lay her head down on her knees as tears fell from her eyes. Evie couldn't remember the last time she had cried so hard. Keeping the water on, she cried until her sobs turned to hiccups.

After a while, she turned the water off and got out of the tub. Wrapping a towel around herself, she went to her dresser, pulled out one of her own t-shirts then took a pair of fresh underwear and got dressed.

She went back into the living room, relieved to see Penni had left.

Going to her purse, she took out her phone and checked the messages. There were three from King and one from Shade. She touched on Shade's message.

"Going hunting. See you soon."

* * *

"Pull up the security tapes from my apartment this morning and get out," King said, walking inside his security room.

Trey pulled up the requested tape then slid his chair back before leaving the room.

King sat in the chair, forwarding the tape to where he wanted it, then pressed play, watching Evie walk into the room. King saw her accidently knock the folder over then she was about to set it back down when he saw her turn toward him in the hallway. King pressed stop, looking at the expression on her face.

She had laid it out for him to see and he had ignored it. He was too used to the betrayals he had suffered through the years.

She hadn't even glanced at the papers in the folders.

Regret filled him at what he had said; he had deliberately pushed her away.

Last night had been the best night he had ever spent with a woman. Hell, the last few weeks were some of the best he'd had in his whole life. Now, he had destroyed her fragile trust with a few well-placed, cruel words.

He took his phone out, calling her, and it was no surprise when she didn't answer his call. He texted her a message instead.

"I'm sorry. Meet me to talk." He sent the message.

It pinged back an hour later with her response. "Fuck off."

Chapter Nineteen

"You're leaving tomorrow?"

"Yes." Evie turned away, putting her dirty dishes in the sink. "I've been here long enough." *Too long*, Evie thought.

As soon as Rabbit had called her and told her Ramos and Moran were heading out of town, she would board her plane.

Rabbit said Ramos had agreed to King's cut, so there actually hadn't been a confrontation between the two men. Evie was relieved King wasn't gaining a new enemy who was trying to move into his territory; he would be able to hand over the reins for the city to the Predators without conflict.

"I have to go to work. Dinner tonight?"

"Sure, I'll even pay," Evie offered.

"Sounds good to me. I'll be back around six."

When Penni left, leaving her with nothing other than time on her hands, she decided to pack. Taking out her cases, she laid them open on the bed. One by one, she emptied the drawers then the closet, leaving out only what she would wear tonight and tomorrow.

When she finished, she looked down at the filled cases,

which held the extent of her possessions. She reached down to a case and pulled out a thin t-shirt, a skimpy blouse, a modest dress, her leather skirt, and one by one, she tossed them to the floor. Evie went into the kitchen and grabbed a trash bag, gathering the clothes into a pile then stuffing them into the bag.

She had almost nothing left, which was what her life felt like at the moment.

Grabbing her purse, she went out the door, locking it behind her. Then, after catching a cab, Evie went shopping.

It wasn't much fun without Jewell, Bliss or Raci, but she picked out the clothes she would need for the next few months. When she finished, she caught a cab back to the apartment. Going through the lobby with her shopping in tow, she didn't take the offer of help from the concierge.

After getting in the elevator, Evie looked down at her watch. She had just enough time to get showered and changed before Penni arrived back from work. She got off the elevator, juggling her bags while searching for her keys. Finally, she found them at the bottom of her purse.

She was so occupied trying to unlock the door with the bags, she didn't notice someone coming up behind her until it was too late. A blinding pain struck at the back of her head, forcing her to her knees, the bags dropping from her hands. She was jerked to her feet by a pair of rough hands and then dragged to the elevator.

Dazed, Evie was slow to react; the doors of the elevator were closing before she was able to begin struggling.

"Stay still, or I will hit you again." Evie felt the barrel of a gun pressed against the back of her skull as the button to the elevator was pushed. "It doesn't matter to me if you're still alive or not as long as King thinks you are."

A rough hand jerked her out of the elevator then into a black SUV that was waiting. Shoving her inside, she fell face-forward into the vehicle.

Evie managed to sit up in the seat with no help from the man who had shoved her inside. He was in his early thirties with brown hair, and the ugly expression on his face let her know he didn't care if she got to their destination breathing or not. She didn't try to make conversation.

Clearly, she'd been lied to about the deal and had been taken to hold over King until it was completed.

She and King had obviously not been discreet the last few weeks. King had been seen with a variety of women over the years and no one had gone after them. His sister had been killed when he was younger, and since then, King had not become close with anyone.

The only reason Evie had been taken was because she was convenient. It was easy to snatch her and blackmail King. However, if Lily had been near, she would have been the target.

Evie's stomach sank. Her kidnapping, whether she lived or died, had sealed King's fate.

* * *

King was in his office when he received the call from Rabbit, passing along Ramos's orders—stay out of the deal. When it was over, Evie would be released. After disconnecting the call, he called Ice.

He had learned a hard lesson several years ago; they had no intention of giving Evie back. She would be used whenever they wanted to use his city. If he didn't comply, she would die.

King went to his security office, calling in reinforcements from there, as well. Afterward, Henry was waiting for him outside. They knew the location of the meeting, and because he was having Evie tailed, they knew where they were keeping her. She was tied up in the same building where the drugs were being sold.

Henry parked the car as close to the location as he could. King and Henry then both got out of the car, using the city they were familiar with to maneuver their way closer.

The car tailing them was being dealt with, so they wouldn't be expecting King to show up. They had put too much faith in King not striking against them because of Evie.

He had backed off when they had taken his sister, and she had been butchered. The same wasn't going to happen to Evie.

King and Henry managed to get close enough to see Ramos and Moran enter the warehouse in different vehicles. Rabbit was inside Moran's car. Rabbit had been the one who had taken Evie to make sure his lucrative cut of the deal was a success. He had been gaining a steady reputation of seeing deals of this caliber involved no bloodshed to those paying for his skills. Unfortunately, he had left a trail of victims like Evie to realize his goals.

Evie had placed too much trust in Rabbit because they had been in the military together. She had also trusted King not to hurt her, afraid of being hurt. Both of them had let her down. She clung to The Last Riders for a reason—she would never have been in this position with the club.

King saw movement behind the warehouse as the Predators moved in. Jackal and Ice were in the lead, giving directions and spreading the men around the warehouse. After Jackal used the darkening sky to get closer to the building, unlocking a side door and going inside, Ice and Max followed behind.

King and Henry used the cars parked outside to hide, making their own way to the door. He reached out to touch the handle when the first shot could be heard from the inside.

"Shit." King jerked opened the door and stepped into Hell without a second's hesitation.

* * *

Evie tried to loosen the tight zip-tie around her wrists, but she quit when two cars pulled into the warehouse. Men climbed out of the cars, holding guns casually by their sides.

Rabbit got out of one, casting a look of apology in her direction. Evie had already figured out he was the one behind her being taken as insurance against King. She had played right into his hands when she had asked for his help in finding out the information she wanted.

Evie was watching as the drugs and money were exchanged when the one who had been left standing guard over her suddenly fell to the concrete floor next to her. Evie stared at him blankly before looking up to see Jackal pulling a knife covered in blood out of the man's back.

When Jackal put his finger to his mouth, telling her without words to remain quiet, Evie nodded her head, showing she understood. Jackal then bent over her chair, cutting the cord at her wrists.

He jerked her from her chair as a bullet struck it, toppling it backward. A small scream passed her lips as Jackal pushed her down to the floor, covering her body with his while grabbing his own gun and returning fire. The men scattered like ants, each running to their own cars.

They didn't make it. They were gunned down steps from their cars. The one who had kidnapped her was one of the first to be killed. Ramos and Moran were each next.

Once their bosses were no longer in control, their men fought unsuccessfully for their own lives. All thirteen of the men were killed. The only one spared was Rabbit, who had hunkered down by the table and didn't move.

When no one was left moving, Jackal helped Evie to her feet. "Are you hurt?"

Evie started to shake her head but dizziness overcame her; only Jackal's hand on her arm kept her from collapsing.

"I was hit on my head."

"Can you walk?"

"Yes."

He didn't take his hand away. "We have to get out of here."

"Evie!" King grabbed her, hugging her close. She tried to move away from him, though. He didn't let her go, yet he allowed her to put some space between them.

"Let me go."

King's arms dropped from her at her cold request.

"King, we need to leave," Jackal ordered. King nodded, stepping back.

It was completely dark when they left the building.

"I'll get the car." Henry jogged off.

"King, thanks for having my back," Rabbit said.

"How did they know about Evie, Rabbit?" Kings harsh voice had Rabbit coming to a stop.

Evie looked at the man she'd thought was her friend. He was going to try to talk his way out of it; it was what made him so good at his job.

The Predators were coming out of the warehouse behind them. Max was carrying the bags containing the drugs and the money.

"What about my cut?" Rabbit asked, as if he had been the one to rescue them.

"You're not—" Evie began angrily.

A shot rang out in the night; Rabbit fell backwards, a hole in the side of his head. The Predators ran for cover, trying to figure out where the shot had come from.

Instinct set in. Evie threw herself into King's arms, pressing against him as tightly as she could. "Don't move!" Evie yelled to everyone around her.

They were under the scope of a cold-blooded killer, and any move they made could be their last.

Chapter Twenty

"Evie..."

"Don't move, King." Evie pressed against him harder.

King's car pulled up to them and he reached out, opening the door. "Get in. If he shoots me, it's what I deserve."

Evie glanced around. The Predators were all escaping, blending into the night. They weren't his target, though; King was. "Get in the car first."

"No."

Evie reluctantly let him go, turning to the direction the shot had come from and staring into the darkness. "Please," she mouthed, no sound escaping. She felt the hair on her arms stand in warning. "Please, don't."

"Evie, get in the car." King was resigned to take his punishment for endangering her, but Evie didn't budge until she saw a brief flash of light and knew she had temporarily bought King a stay. Only then did she finally slide into the car with her head pounding.

King closed the car door, lighting a cigar with a shaking hand. "Do you need to go to the hospital?"

"No, I have a concussion. I need to lie down and take

it easy for a while, but I will be fine. I guess I won't be catching my plane in the morning."

"You booked a plane? You were going to leave without talking to me?"

"I have nothing to say."

"Evie, I'm sorry I jumped to conclusions."

"You're full of shit. You've judged me from the moment you met me, just like you did Shade. You're the one who's fucked up. I trusted you. I thought you were smart enough to step away from that deal. I was wrong. The next time you screw up, I won't be around to save your ass."

"I did step away. I told Ramos to do his business and get out of town, then Rabbit called and said Ramos had you. He didn't trust me not to interfere. I spent most of my life building my reputation, and it almost got you killed!"

"Thank God, it wasn't Lily."

"You're just as important as Lily is to me, Evie."

"Don't lie," Evie seethed.

"I'm not lying."

Evie turned away, not willing to argue with him. That's when she noticed Henry had pulled up in front of King's building. "Take me to Penni's."

"Stay the night. At least let me make sure you're okay. You can sleep in the spare bedroom. You have to be checked every so often because of your concussion."

"Penni is there."

"You want to explain to her what happened?"

No, she didn't. It would be hours before Penni would let her sleep if she did.

Resigned to her fate, Evie tiredly got out of the car, moving away from King's touch. Silently, she followed him into his penthouse. She knew the way to his spare bedroom and that's where she went, closing the door on him before he could speak.

She toed off her shoes before lying down on the bed,

not bothering to turn down the blankets. Curling on her side, she stared at the emptiness of the bed beside her and fell asleep within minutes. She hadn't slept through the night since her fight with King.

Later that night, King woke her up with a cold drink. When she sat up, gratefully taking a long gulp, he gave her some ibuprofen which helped with her headache.

She was about to go back to sleep when she realized she didn't have her purse. She started to get out of bed.

"What are you doing?"

"I need my purse; it has my phone."

"You're going to leave in the middle of the night for your phone?"

"I need my phone," she said stubbornly.

"Get back in bed. I'll send Henry after it."

"Thank you." Evie lay back down, falling back asleep.

* * *

Sometime later, she felt her head prodded.

"Stop, that hurts!"

"Let him check you out."

Evie's eyes flickered open to see an older face staring down at her interestedly.

"Hello," he said.

"Hi."

"He's my physician," King said. "I wanted to have you checked out to make sure you're okay."

"It's just a mild concussion."

"She's right," King's physician agreed, straightening from the bed.

"Told you so," Evie muttered then fell back asleep.

* * *

Evie woke feeling more clearheaded later in the day. She sat up slowly before getting to her feet, making sure she wasn't dizzy before going to the bathroom. She took her time washing her face, staring at her pale reflection; the dark shadows under her eyes would need a coat of make-up to cover them.

Back in the bedroom, she flipped through her messages then texted Penni she was fine and would be back that afternoon. She then called and rescheduled her flight, giving herself a couple of days before she traveled.

She looked down at the t-shirt she was wearing, surprised. She hadn't imagined King would ever own a t-shirt; it didn't fit his elegant style. She couldn't picture him in jeans and t-shirts. He was the complete antithesis of the type of men who attracted her.

She picked up her clothes from the chair, getting dressed, and King came in as she was putting on her shoes.

"What are you doing?"

"Leaving. I'm feeling better."

"Stay. You need to recuperate."

"I can do that at Penni's."

He stood with his hands in his pockets, staring back at her with a grim face. "I can't convince you to stay?"

"No." Evie picked up her phone and purse, ready to leave the close confines of the bedroom. She stared back at him coldly as he blocked her exit.

"Evie, I know I fucked up."

"How many times do I have to tell you I don't want to talk?"

"Haven't you ever screwed up, Evie?"

"Not when I give my loyalty to someone. Loyalty is everything." She touched the tattoo on the curve of her breast. "I hurt Beth *one* time, and I will *always* regret it. I did it because I was loyal to The Last Riders. I broke that loyalty—men who have stood beside me for years—for you. They deserve my loyalty; you do not." Evie walked past him into the living room.

"I'll call Henry."

As Evie heard the defeat in his voice, she wanted to turn around and hide in his arms. The last thing she wanted to do was leave him, but he had showed her he didn't trust her. He had been pretending to care for her to find out a way to hurt her friends, and he had almost succeeded.

While they stood, awkwardly waiting for Henry's arrival, her eyes roved to the television screen behind King's shoulder. There was a breaking news report describing the violence of the last twenty-four hours. They were detailing the gruesome discovery of several bodies at the warehouse, then the shocking execution-style killing of Digger as he was being moved to a safe house. King stared along with Evie as they watched Digger's sheet-covered body loaded into the coroner's van.

"I would have paid him for that one myself," King commented, not making eye contact.

"It wasn't for you." It was for Lily; it would always be about Lily for Shade.

King's phone rang, announcing Henry's arrival downstairs.

King walked her to the elevator and Evie felt the tension climb, sensing King wanted her to stay. However, when the elevator opened, Evie stepped in, her finger pressing the lobby button. "Goodbye, King."

His hand stopped the elevator from closing. "I know you hate me right now, and I don't blame you. I asked for your trust without giving you mine. I was wrong. It wasn't the first time I was wrong dealing with you, though, and I'm sure it won't be the last. My sister was murdered because I trusted someone's word I shouldn't have, and she paid the price.

"I've made no secret of the fact that I don't like Shade, and I was well aware your loyalty to him came first. Last night, you threw yourself in front of me to save me from him. Whether you know it or not, you made a decision to pick me over The Last Riders.

"I'm moving to Treepoint, but it's going to take me some time to finish up here. That will give you some time to cool down and come to the same realization I have—we belong together. We are fucking good together. And neither you nor The Last Riders are going to keep me from proving I can be worthy of your loyalty. I'll see you in a few weeks."

Evie didn't say anything, letting the elevator door close on the man she had come to love.

* * *

Three days later, her bags were packed once more. Evie stared down at the new suitcases she had purchased containing new clothes. The only things leaving with her she had brought were The Last Riders' t-shirts she used to sleep in. She had also purchased a couple of nightshirts in different colors.

"I'll see you this summer when I come in for the Fourth of July picnic." Penni hugged her.

"Take care, Penni." Evie picked up her suitcase, opening the door. "Be careful around the Predators."

"I will. I have no intention of becoming involved with them." Evie looked at her doubtfully. While Penni was trying her best to avoid the Predators, she hoped her antagonism for them remained strong. She was glad Penni was in and out of town, touring with Mouth2Mouth.

"Bye, Evie."

"Goodbye, Penni," she said with finality, going out the door.

She blinked back tears in her eyes. She was going to miss Penni. They had grown close the last several weeks living together.

Wheeling her suitcase out of the elevator, she stopped at the concierge desk. The new employee had been hired when the old one had let the man kidnap her onto the elevator for a large tip.

Evie reached into her purse, pulling out a thick envelope.

"Keep an eye on her. If you see she's in any kind of trouble, call the number in the envelope. It's her brother."

"I will. Thanks, Evie."

She nodded, handing him the envelope of money before rolling her suitcase outside where the taxi she had called was waiting. The driver put her suitcase in the trunk while Evie climbed into the car. The driver slammed the trunk then got back behind the wheel.

"The airport," Evie said, looking out the window with tears brimming in her eyes.

"Where you headed?" he asked, pulling out into the heavy traffic.

"I'm going home."

Chapter Twenty-one

The taxi pulled up in front of the small house. It was well-maintained with a pretty, grassy yard and spring flowers blossoming, lining the white picket fence.

Evie got out of the cab while the driver got her suitcase. Taking it from him, she turned toward the house then headed up the sidewalk. She bent down next to a decorative rock, and turning it over, she located the key Beth had promised to leave for her.

Evie unlocked the front door and stepped inside, pausing inside the doorway to turn on the lights since the shades were all drawn.

"Welcome home, Evie," she said out loud to herself, staring around the empty house.

Beth and Lily had cleaned out all their things, and Evie had signed the papers the day before she left for Texas.

"Enjoy your trip?" Evie stiffened when she heard the voice behind her.

Turning around, she kept her face an expressionless mask. "Brooke, what do you want?"

"Can't I come by and say hello to my sister?"

"You're not my sister."

Her fake laughter sounded off the empty walls. "I saw your taxi driving by as I was coming out of the church. Not much goes on in this sleepy, little town, does it?"

"Then leave. Go back to New York. Hell, go home to Georgia; I'm sure Mom misses you." Evie was proud of the lack of resentment in her voice.

"Aren't you getting too old to still be jealous of mine and mom's relationship?"

"I'm not jealous at all; you two are just alike."

"Let's not start that again. I came by to say hello. It's time we started being sisters again. Twins are supposed to be close." Her hand rubbed over the baby bump that had grown in size since she had left.

"We may have been fraternal twins, but we have never been close. You made sure of that, Brooke, not me."

"Don't tell me you're still holding a grudge?"

Evie's face whitened. "It's because of you I was raped! Did you think I would ever forgive you? You had Thompson wrapped around your finger. He was the one who egged those men on when we got back to base."

"I did not."

"Don't fucking lie about it anymore, Brooke. He told Shade the truth. The dumb fuck would have done anything to make you happy. He called you when we got back to base, told you how the men were treating me. Then, when they started drinking, you told him to take his friends to my quarters. You told them I put out enough in high school that I would enjoy it." Evie was practically screaming at her.

Brooke's face didn't change expression, but Evie could see from the malicious gleam in her eyes that she was accomplishing her goal of upsetting her. Brooke had always pushed her buttons; she did it deliberately to get the reaction she wanted. Her twin was sick; that was why Evie had joined the Navy, to escape her influence when her mother had refused to see the truth.

"I was a virgin. You knew that, yet you sent those men

after me."

"How was I to know you were still a virgin? You and Shade were constantly together in high school. You joined the Navy together. You, Shade and Levi. The three of you were together all the time," Brooke mocked her, the hatred she felt blazing from her eyes.

"You couldn't take it, could you, Brooke? I told you there wasn't anything between me and Shade. You knew I was in love with Levi, that we were going to get married when we got out of the service." Evie briefly closed her eyes.

The friendship the three had shared had been strong. Evie and Levi had been high school sweethearts. When Shade had come to their school their junior year, he and Levi had become friends. The three of them had become close, going on double dates, sharing dreams, and graduating together. Afterwards, the three of them had decided to join the Navy together.

"But it was Shade you were constantly talking to, it was his shoulder you cried on when you were raped, and it was his house you went to when you were discharged." Brooke was almost screaming at her, her face turning an ugly color of red.

"How could I go home, Brooke? You had already convinced Mom it was all my fault, that I had made those charges up. After Levi died, I had no reason to go back to Georgia, did I?"

"You're going to blame me for Levi's death, too?"

I'm not going to lose control, Evie kept telling herself over and over.

"No, that was his fault. I told him to stay away from Thompson and his friends. I warned him they wouldn't fight fair, and they didn't. Thompson sucker-punched him; his falling and hitting his head was an accident."

Evie could still remember Shade's face when he had come into her bedroom while she was staying with his mom and Penni. She had known it was bad before he had even opened his mouth. The horror of Levi's death still gave her nightmares. She had once felt she'd been the reason he had died; it had taken Shade a long time to convince her she hadn't been responsible.

When Lily had hit her head during the robbery in Sex Piston's shop and had nearly died, it had brought the pain of losing Levi back to both her and Shade. She had heard how violently he had reacted at the hospital and had wished she could have been there to help him as he had been there for her over the last seven years.

Evie walked across the room, raising the blinds to let the sun inside. Moving to the next window, she raised those blinds, as well, wishing Brooke would just leave. However, she wouldn't leave until she came to say whatever it was she considered important enough to confront Evie with.

"What do you want, Brooke?"

"I want to make peace between us; you, me and Shade."

It dawned on Evie then exactly why Brooke was there. "Please, don't tell me you haven't given up the hope of getting Shade. For God's sake, Brooke, you're pregnant with Merrick's baby!"

"This was an accident, and one I don't intend to let affect my life. Besides, many men find women attractive when they're pregnant."

Evie stared at her sister in disgust. "How have you managed to hide your true colors from Merrick?"

"Merrick only sees the good in everyone."

"He must to be married to you. Although, the Lord knows I've tried unsuccessfully to find anything redeemable in you, so I'm not sure where *he* finds it."

Brooke looked down at her watch. "I need to get back to the church. I've offered to help Lily in the store this afternoon."

Evie's blood ran cold.

"Do not mess with Lily."

"I never expected Shade to end up with someone so meek and mild. She was quite a surprise. I never even expected him to be married, so it was quite a shock when she was introduced to me. Dean didn't tell Merrick because he didn't know we were sisters, which, by the way, caused me to have a lot of explaining to do to Merrick."

Evie could only imagine the fake look of innocence on Brooke's face as she had lied to her husband. Brooke had always managed to make Evie look like she was jealous and resentful of her.

"Whatever it is you're thinking of doing, I wouldn't, Brooke. Shade is never going to have anything to do with you—he hates you more than I do—and if you try to hurt Lily, you'll see a side of him you never imagined existed."

Brooke actually shuddered in anticipation at her warning. "You really are sick!" Evie said.

For a brief moment, Brooke's face twisted into a mask of hatred. "I told you years ago he was mine, but you didn't listen to me, Evie. You turned him against me. Well, he'll see me in a whole different light now. You'll see."

"No, he won't. He loves Lily."

"For now. There isn't much I can do until after the baby is born anyway." Brooke turned toward the door. "You really need to get some furniture. I believe the church store has a few pieces sitting around." With that, Brooke sauntered out the door.

Evie wanted to slam it shut and lock it behind her. Instead, she closed it softly, not wanting to give Brooke the satisfaction of hearing Evie's anger.

She raised the windows, letting the fresh air in to relieve the room of Brooke's cloying perfume and fill the house with a faint breeze after it had been sitting empty since being broken into before Lily and Shade had gotten married.

Evie was about to pack her suitcase upstairs when she heard the roar of motors coming down the street. She didn't wait for them to come to the house; she flung the door open, running outside. Jewel and Raci jumped off the backs of the bikes they were riding on.

"Why didn't you call? We would have picked you up at the airport," Jewell complained.

"I didn't want to get you guys in trouble for missing work. I know what a slave-driver Shade can be," she teased as Shade sat watching the commotion of her greeting everyone from his bike.

"How did you know I was back? I was getting ready to call."

"I saw you when the security alarm went off," Shade stated matter-of-factly while his eyes searched her face.

"I forgot to key in the code."

"Your visitor must have distracted you." Her eyes were caught by his; he had seen on the camera and came.

"She didn't stay long."

"Who stopped by?" Jewell asked curiously.

"No one important." She had never shared any of her past with any of the women of The Last Riders, even though the men all knew because they had been her support and crutch when it had all happened.

Knowing better than to push for answers Evie wasn't going to give, they all filed inside her new home.

"So, what's first?" Raci stared around the empty room.

"The first thing is the furniture store. Want to go with me?"

Raci, Jewell and Ember all agreed to go while the men were going to head back to the clubhouse.

"You going to come by tonight?" Train slung an arm around her shoulder.

"Not tonight. I'm tired from the trip and want to get unpacked," Evie replied evasively, moving away slightly. Train's frown had her smiling. "I'll be there for work bright and early tomorrow, though, so don't worry."

"It wasn't work I was thinking about. I've missed having you around." Evie smiled at him; that was quite an admission from Train.

"I missed you guys, too," Evie admitted.

"If we're going to get this house furnished, we need to get to the store," Raci reminded her.

"I'm coming." Beth had dropped Evie's car off for her yesterday and had left the keys on the kitchen counter. Picking them up, Evie grinned at her friends.

"Let's go spend some money," the women yelled while the men groaned as everyone trailed out of the house.

Shade was the last one out the door and waited for her to lock it. "Brooke cause any problems?"

"Same old Brooke. What can I say? Shade, she's really sick. I can't believe she's my sister."

"She's not sick; she's an evil bitch. I wish I had known who she was married to; I would have talked Lucky out of letting Merrick take over for him."

"It's too late now. We'll just have to deal with her."

Shade turned to walk back to his bike, but Evie grabbed his arm. "Shade, she's still fixated on you. Watch out. I'm worried with Lily being around her so often."

Shade's face darkened. "I didn't want to talk to Lily about Brooke until I spoke with you first."

Evie sighed. "You're going to have to tell her everything. I understand. I don't want her hurt because you want to respect my privacy."

"Are you sure?"

"Yes. Lily won't talk about my past with anyone, and she of all people will understand me not wanting to talk about it."

"I'll talk to her tonight."

"The sooner, the better. I don't want to give Brooke any opportunity to damage what you and Lily have."

"If that bitch causes you any more problems, you tell me immediately."

"I will. I promise."

Shade gave her a brief nod before going to his bike.

The women were yelling at her to hurry, hanging out Rider's truck window. Evie smiled, rushing across the grassy lawn toward them.

"It's good to be home," she told them, jumping up into the truck.

"It's about time," Jewell said, scooting over to make room. "I thought you were going to be gone a couple of weeks, not months. What kept you?"

"I needed to take care of some club business. It took longer than we thought, but now I'm back and I'm not leaving you guys again."

"Thank fuck. Guess who's cooking dinner tomorrow night for everyone?" Raci laughed.

Evie groaned. She had missed her friends, not the cooking duties.

Putting the truck in gear, she drove to the furniture store as she listened contently to the chatter around her. This was where she belonged now, surrounded by her friends and The Last Riders. She wouldn't forget that ever again.

Chapter Twenty-two

"We've got a problem." King looked up from the computer screen at Henry's comment.

"Does it have to do with the club?"

"Yeah."

"Then it's your problem. I'm leaving in two days. The papers are signed. It's now your club, your problem." He looked back down at the computer screen.

"Fine, I'll tell Penni to fuck off. Since she's Shade's sister, I kind of figured that made you related."

"No, it doesn't," King rebutted then gave an aggravated sigh. He owed the woman; she had watched out for Lily during their college years. "What's the problem?"

"She won't tell me; she wants to talk with you. She's waiting downstairs."

"You left her downstairs on her own with the club busy?"

"Yeah, the woman has an attitude."

"What did she do to piss you off?" King read the frustration in Henry's face.

"She offered Sherri a job as her assistant, told her she

deserved better than shaking her ass on a stage for a bunch of horny old men."

King almost laughed but understood why Henry was upset; Sherri was their top earner, and one of Henry's personal favorites.

Getting to his feet, he went to the door. "You do know that eventually she's going to move on." King stopped when he saw the twisted expression of pain on his friend's face at his casual comment.

"She wouldn't want me; I'm too old and ugly. She's going with Max now, anyways."

"Max will have someone new in a couple of weeks. When he breaks it off with her, ask her out. She'll go out with you."

"You think so?"

"Yes." King opened the door and went out with Henry following.

Going downstairs, he came to a full stop when he saw what was going on. Penni was sitting at the bar, surrounded by his workers who should be waiting on the men in the club or dancing.

"I better see what she wants before we don't have anyone left working for us. Send her over." King sat down at his booth, watching as Henry took Penni's arm and led her across the room.

"Hi, King." He found himself returning the unaffected smile the woman gave. Penni was as boisterous as Lily was quiet and reserved.

"Henry told me you're trying to steal my workers."

"I think everyone deserves options, don't you?"

"They have options, just none that can bring them the kind of money I can."

"So I heard. Sherri was interested until I told her the pay scale." She shrugged, unconcerned.

King noticed at that point that Ice, Jackal and Max came in through the door. They went to the end of the bar closest to his booth, unashamedly listening to their conversation.

Penni turned her head to see what King was staring at. Her blue eyes might be the same color as her brother's, but his always remained expressionless while Penni's showed every emotion she was feeling. Right now, they were spewing hatred at Jackal who was leaning sideways against the bar, facing the table with a beer in his hand.

"What can I help you with, Penni?" King drew her attention back to him.

"I heard you're going back to Treepoint."

King stiffened. "How did you hear that?"

"Vida, of course. Why? Is there a problem with me knowing?"

"I didn't want to advertise where I am moving to. It's safer for Lily that way."

Penni waved her hand, unconcerned. "You don't have to worry about that. I won't say anything. I can keep a secret." She gave him a wink.

King blasted Ice with a look for letting the information out. Colton was a member of the Predators who had obviously confided in his wife, Vida, of King's plans to leave Queen City. Ice shrugged, silently telling him Vida, Sawyer and Penni weren't his problem.

"I would appreciate it." King motioned for the bartender to bring him a drink; he had a feeling he was going to need it before he could get rid of Penni.

"Anyway, Evie left something behind for me, and I've decided I don't want it. Could you give it back to her for me?"

"Yes."

"Thanks." King watched as she then dug in her large bag. He expected her to pull out a pair of earrings, not the forty-five revolver she whipped out and slapped down on the table between them.

"Whoa," Jackal said, spilling his beer.

"Motherfucker," Ice said, his hand going behind his back.

King lifted his hand to Ice, stopping him, while glaring at Henry to step back.

"She left it for me to use as protection, but I nearly shot my date last night when we went back to my apartment. I forgot it was under the couch cushion." Her red face told exactly how she had been reminded of its presence.

King picked it up from the table. Thankfully, the safety was on, so he simply placed it in his suit pocket.

"I'll see she gets it back." He would give it back to her along with some strong words for letting Penni have it in the first place.

"I appreciate it. I found something that will work that isn't so big." When she lifted her purse and started to look through it again, Jackal took the purse away from her.

"Give that back!" Penni yelled, beginning to get up. Instead, Jackal pushed her back in the booth, sitting down next to her while going through her purse. King saw her smug smile as he searched her purse. He raised a brow when Jackal came up empty-handed.

Penni jerked her purse back, reaching inside. When she pulled out her car keys, both men looked at them, stumped at how keys could be used as a weapon.

"You going to strangle them with the cord?" Jackal asked, amused. Her car keys hung from a nylon cord with a tiny ball at the end, wrapped in the cord.

"May I?" Penni asked him. King nodded, interested to see if she would try to use it to strangle Jackal, who was still laughing at her.

After Penni held the car keys in her hand and swung the ball at the table, Jackal quit laughing. King grabbed his drink at the thump the ball made against the table.

"If someone tries to bother me, I'll hit them with this. It's supposed to knock them out."

King closed his mouth, looking at the innocuous ball. It could be a deadly weapon if used by the right hand. King narrowed his eyes on Penni. The exuberant woman hid a vicious streak. She reminded King of a pet one of his strippers had several years ago. Sheena had a pet chimpanzee she had trained to take off her top during her act. The men had loved it. Everyone thought it was adorable right up until the moment the little fucker had bitten off two of Sheena's fingers.

"I can see that." King reached out, picking up the ball from the table. It was a metal ball bearing underneath the wrapped cord. If swung with enough force at a man's temple, the damage could be permanent.

"So, like I said, you can tell Evie I don't need the gun," Penni said happily, picking her keys back up from the table.

King started laughing, unable to help himself. He should have known that if she was related to Shade, she would have a hidden side to her.

"What's so funny?" Penni asked suspiciously.

"Nothing. I'll give her your message."

"Thanks. Give Lily a kiss for me." When her facial expression changed instantly, King knew the two had a deep friendship.

"I want to thank you for being such a good friend to her."

"She's like a sister to me, King."

"Has she—" King cleared his throat. "Does she ever talk about me?"

"King, if you need answers from Lily, the best person to ask is her." Penni wouldn't betray any of Lily's confidences, but he had hoped to find out if she had discussed her feelings of him being in her life.

"I'll do that."

"Good. She's a special person. I'm happy she's my sister-in-law."

Penni moved to get out, yet was forestalled by Jackal, who was blocking her exit.

"Who did you go out with?" Jackal's question took the smile off Penni's lips.

"No one you would know. He's a gentleman and a law-abiding citizen, something you would know nothing about," she snapped.

Jackal gave a menacing glare. "Why would I want to be either one? The only pussy a gentleman sees is when he's staring in a mirror. Are you throwing up my record when your own brother—"

"Don't you dare say anything about my brother!" She leaned forward, putting her face in his. "He's a better man than you could ever be, you goon!"

Jackal's face darkened with fury. "Did you just call me a goon?"

"Something wrong with your hearing? Yeah, I called you a goon. Do you do everything Ice tells you to?" Penni blasted Ice with a furious glare. "Do me a favor and tell Jackal to go fuck himself."

"How about I stick my—" Jackal snarled, getting back in Penni's face.

"Jackal!" King gave him a warning look. "Perhaps you and Ice should go have a drink on me."

For a minute, King thought Jackal would ignore him, yet when Ice took his arm, Jackal got up, moving away. To add insult to injury, Penni wiggled her fingers "bye" at his being forced to retreat by Ice.

"I wouldn't antagonize him," King advised.

"I can handle Jackal," she said, gripping her keys tighter in her hand and then shrugging, letting the tension leave her face. "And if I can't, there's always Shade to back me up."

"He's in Kentucky," he reminded Penni. "Jackal is here in Texas."

"Don't worry, King. I plan on staying away from him." She stood up. He was startled when she reached over the table, giving him a brief hug. "Talk to Lily. Maybe she's just as nervous as you are."

"I doubt that," he said wryly.

Her bubbly laughter filled the dark club, bringing

smiles to several faces.

"Take her some Chinese food. She loves it."

"Thanks for the tip."

"No problem." With that, Penni left him with the first smile he'd had on his face since before Evie had left Queen City.

Glancing over, he saw the predatory look on Jackal's face as the blonde weaved her way out of his club. The experienced biker and womanizer had no idea who he was stalking. King briefly thought about giving him a heads-up, but Sheena hadn't listened when he had warned her about that crazy chimp she had pampered and spoiled until it was too late. Therefore, if Jackal thought he was man enough to take on that woman, King could only hope he had 911 on speed dial.

"Sure you don't want to stay?" Henry asked from his side.

"I'm sure. Keep an eye on that situation." He nodded at Penni as she went out the door. "If it gets out of hand, call me."

"She'll be fine," Henry assured him.

"It's not Penni I'm worried about. Jackal has a temper, and she's used to dealing with a brother who doesn't have emotions. Jackal is a hot-head, so when she pushes him, she'll get more than she bargained for."

"I'll keep an eye on them," Henri promised. "You packed?"

"Yes, I was ready to leave a week ago." King sighed. He had one last piece of business to finish. He nodded to Ice and Jackal who took a seat across from him.

"You talk to Deacon?" King asked the president of the Predators.

"I did; I warned him to back off Desmond." Desmond had angered Deacon when he had bought a building Deacon wanted. While the two had been business enemies for the last three years, King had always managed to maintain the peace between them. However, now he was leaving, he worried Deacon would make a strike against Desmond.

"Did he listen?"

"He pretended to, even shook my hand and told me he would leave Desmond alone," Ice stated. "Do I trust his word? Fuck no. I've placed a couple of my men on him, so if he tries anything, we'll be on him like Max on Sherri." The bikers laughed while Henry stiffened next to him.

King rubbed his temple. It was essential for Henry and the Predators to get along or Queen City would be out of control ten minutes after he left town.

"Max has four kids, all accidents. Desmond better not get hurt because of lack of precautions," Henry said drily.

King watched Ice and Jackal's reaction as the men gave Henry a respectful nod. His final doubt over whether Henry would be able to retain control evaporated. The bikers were aware that, with Henry and Desmond, they could keep Queen City in a stranglehold that would be lucrative to all of them.

He had chosen Henry as his bodyguard for a reason—he was able to spot trouble before it could do any damage. If the Predators and Desmond listened to Henry, he would be able to provide them with all the information they needed. The strip club catered to all walks of life, and men would let secrets drop when a beautiful woman was flashing her tits in their face.

He sat back, relaxing. He would miss his club and Queen City, but neither compared to being nearer to Evie and Lily. He was going to have to find a new challenge to keep him occupied.

Chapter Twenty-three

As King drove through town, he saw that church service was beginning with the congregation entering the front of the Church. He didn't see Lily or Evie, so he continued on to the house he had purchased years ago.

It didn't take long to get situated. He had unpacked his suitcase before he'd tackled the job of opening the windows to let the house freshen out. He was turning from the window after opening it when movement in the house behind his caught his eye. Looking out the window, he saw Evie come out of Lily's house wearing a bikini and carrying a glass in her hand. He watched as she walked across the yard, sitting down on a lounge chair.

Why was she there? He had expected her to be at church.

Turning from the window, he went out the back door; there was no time like the present to let her know he was in town. It had been three months since he had seen her last. Three months of being away from her had taught him a valuable lesson—he didn't want to spend another day without her.

He was finally free to pursue the woman who had left him without a backward glance. He had asked Lily about Evie, but the only information she had given him had been vague and incomplete, other than she no longer worked at the factory after accepting a job at a local doctor's office as a NP.

He walked around the fence, seeing the opening between the two yards that a tree blocked.

She was lying down on the lounger on her back.

"Are you wearing any sunscreen?"

"That would defeat the purpose of lying out for a tan, wouldn't it?" Her stiff voice showed she wasn't happy to see him.

King ignored her smart-ass remark, pulling a chair from the patio table to move closer to her. Taking a seat, he lazily let his eyes rove over her glistening body.

"What are you wearing?" She sat up partially, leaning back on her elbows.

His eyes dropped to her breasts displayed by the bikini top she was wearing. The emerald green suit clung to her breasts, leaving her cleavage bare. The sight of her tattoo on her breast no longer aroused his jealousy, though. He had learned too late that, while she had shared her body with certain members of The Last Riders, she hadn't given her heart to any of them. That had been reserved for a fiancé she had grown up with and now him, if he could get her back.

The only thought that made the months he had been separated from her bearable was the fact that Evie didn't love lightly, and loyalty meant everything to her, even when it wasn't deserved. He didn't deserve it, but he was going to prove to her he was willing to earn it.

"Jeans. Why?"

"Since when do you wear jeans?"

"I've worn jeans around you before."

"Yeah, designer jeans. Those are blue jeans and a t-shirt."

"I'm retired. I can relax."

Evie stared up at him doubtfully.

"It's the truth. I've turned my legal businesses over to

Desmond. Those that aren't, the Predators took over. I even sold the club to Henry."

"What about your penthouse?"

"I leased it out for the next six months until you decide where you want to live."

She sat up straighter, swinging her legs off the side of the lounge chair. "What does it matter what I want? If you cared about what I wanted, your ass wouldn't be sitting in my backyard."

"I would have been here sooner, but I wanted to make sure I could leave cleanly. I took care of anything that could lead back to you and Lily."

"Good, I'm glad for Lily's sake." She avoided his eyes.

"Evie, I admitted I fucked up with you. I know you don't believe me, but I care about you, and I want us to spend some time getting to know each other better without my business and The Last Riders placing a wall between us."

"You want me to believe you've accepted Shade as Lily's husband?"

"Evie, you have to place yourself in my shoes. You turn a blind eye to what he does, but you have to admit he's not the average man."

"I wouldn't describe him as average, no." King smiled at her mutinous response.

"I had him checked out, Evie; we both know what he is capable of. I couldn't stand the thought of her getting hurt again and just standing back, doing nothing. I should have done better by Lily, but I waited until I had no choice other than to change the path I was walking. It took her almost getting killed to realize I was going to have to leave that life behind.

"I don't only want a future with Lily, though; I want you, too, Evie. If it means accepting Shade as her husband, then I'm willing to accept your opinion that they're right for each other. I don't see it, but she does and so do you. What's important to me now is you. I've made my mind up; I'm going to let Lily live her life while I make a new one for me. One that I can be proud of; one that includes you."

"I don't know, King."

"Come out to dinner with me tonight?"

"I'll think about it," she hedged.

King stood up. "I'll pick you up at seven."

"I didn't say yes!"

"You didn't say no, either." He bent down, brushing her mouth with his then swiftly moving away before she could voice her protest. "We'll go to the Pink Slipper. See you at seven."

King left the same way he'd come, whistling softly as he crossed the yard, relieved she was at least talking to him. He was satisfied he had made a start in repairing the damage he had done, repairing the fledgling relationship that had been building in Queen City.

* * *

Evie sat staring at the opening in the fence King had disappeared through. She had lost her ever-freaking mind to even consider going out with him that evening.

Lying back down on the lounger, she closed her eyes against the bright sunlight. Sighing, she admitted to herself she had missed his overwhelming presence; therefore, she could keep being angry at him or accept his apology and move on. One tiny voice in her head muttered to stay angry while another, more insidious voice undermined her resolve, whispering to forgive the man she had fallen in love with. There really wasn't a choice; she could take another chance or keep missing him.

As she rolled to her stomach, letting the sun bake her back, she heard cars coming down the street outside her house. Church must have been over. No one but Lily and Shade understands why she no longer went; she wanted to avoid everyone's questions. However, she missed going. The Sunday practice had become a ritual. Next week, she would drive to Jamestown to the Baptist church there.

171

She wasn't the only one who had quit going since Lucky had quit being a pastor, though. Willa no longer went, either. Evie would have to ask her if she wanted to ride to the other church with her.

She had been able to avoid Brooke since she had been back because working for Dr. Jones had kept her busy. She felt content and happy with the changes she had made in her life. She still hung out some days at the clubhouse, but it was no longer the focus of her life. She had finally learned to sleep through the night without having to exhaust herself with sex and liquor to numb the pain of losing Levi. She no longer used sex as a way to prove to herself those men who had raped her hadn't damaged her. She hadn't had sex with anyone since she had been back, yet the surprising part was she hadn't been tempted.

The memory of King had been holding her back. She couldn't forget the times she had spent in his bed. She also couldn't remember who she had fucked last when she had left the clubhouse before heading out for Queen City. The stark reality of the situation was, she didn't need The Last Riders to keep being her crutch; she had learned to stand alone.

When Levi had died, she had needed them to heal her to make her feel safe and give her back her sexuality. King had accomplished the rest of her healing—he had taught her to love again.

She wanted more now. She wanted what Lily and Shade had, what Knox and Diamond had. When she saw Beth's pregnancy becoming more and more noticeable, she ached inside; she wanted a baby most of all.

When she and Levi had planned their marriage, they had talked of children. They had planned two, but secretly, she had wanted four. She wasn't going to have children if she held on to her anger. She had to forgive King or move on, and tonight would help her make up her mind.

Beginning to feel like she was getting sunburned, she went inside to make herself some lunch. She ate until she heard the doorbell ring, only opening the door when she saw it was Lily outside.

"I wanted to stop by and see you since you weren't in church today."

Evie opened the door wider, letting her in. She didn't make up false reasons why she hadn't gone. "I think the best way for me and Brooke to get along is to stay away from each other. Would you like a glass of tea?"

"Thank you." Lily sat down on the sofa while Evie went into the kitchen to pour them some tea.

She placed it on the coffee table in front of Lily before dropping down next to her. "So, what are you really doing here?"

"I wanted to see if you would throw Beth a baby shower." She rushed on, "I know as her sister I should, but Shade and baby showers don't mix, and I promised him after Sex Piston's I wouldn't throw another one. Of course, when I promised, I didn't know Beth would be pregnant a few months later."

"I would love to. When?"

Lily shrugged happily. "That's up to you. She's due the last of August."

"I'll get right on it then." Evie smiled.

"Good. I wasn't looking forward to trying to convince Shade."

"I don't think you would have too big a battle; he's the happiest I've ever seen him. I saw him riding home from taking you to the church store on Friday, and he had an actual smile on his face."

Lily's violet eyes were so much like her father's that Evie paused, staring at her.

"What?"

"You resemble your dad."

"I noticed." Tentatively, she probed, "When you were in Queen City with Penni, did you see King?" Neither Lily nor Evie had ever broached the subject of her stay in Texas.

"Yes, we went out a few times."

"I'm glad. I worried about you being lonely while you were there because I've noticed Penni can stay busy, getting wrapped up in her own world. I'm happy you and King kept each other company."

Evie licked her lips. "Would it bother you if I started seeing your dad, now that he's back in town?"

"King's in Treepoint?"

"Yes, you didn't know?"

"No, I guess he made his presence known to the most important one," she teased.

"I'm sure he knew you were in church." Evie began to explain in case Lily's feelings were hurt.

Lily laughed, shaking her head. "He didn't have any problem finding you, did he? Don't worry, Evie; I'm not upset. Why wouldn't I want you to see King?"

"Because of The Last Riders."

"Evie, I'm not going to judge your behavior with the men and women at the clubhouse, if that's what you're expecting. Do I seem selfish to you?"

"No, why?"

"Because I want you to be as happy as I am." Lily took her hand.

Evie stared back at the most unselfish person she had ever known. Lily truly was a kindhearted woman. Brooke would make mincemeat out of her if given half a chance, and Evie couldn't let that happen.

"Lily, Shade told you about Brooke, right?"

"That she's your sister, and you had a falling out. He said she's had a thing for him, and he thinks she's mentally disturbed." From the blush on Lily's cheeks, Evie was certain those weren't the exact words Shade had used.

"Don't trust her, Lily. She would hurt you and not blink twice." Evie's hand curled around Lily's, trying to make her understand how seriously she should take the warning.

"I'll be careful. Shade's already made me promise not

to be alone with her. It's not easy with me working at the church, though. And I really like Pastor Patterson. I can't imagine going to another church, and I love my job. Do you think it's possible she's changed?"

"Not a chance in hell."

Chapter Twenty-four

Evie was waiting when King rang the doorbell, frustrated at herself for being so anxious. She had dressed early and much dressier than the occasion called for. Nervously, she answered the door, waiting for his reaction.

"Evie, you look beautiful." He took her hands, pulling her forward until she felt herself pressed against him. His ruthless mouth took hers, kissing all her misgivings away while giving her new ones to worry about.

"Want to forget dinner?" His eyes slid appreciatively over her body.

She pressed her hands against his chest, giving herself some breathing room. "No, I haven't decided if I'm going to forgive you today or tomorrow or ever."

Evie shrugged into her peach jacket, covering her little black dress with a gold belt. She was wearing a pair of black sandals that had cutouts all the way to her ankles. She thought she looked poised and elegant while still having a trace of attitude.

King was back in his familiar suit, which Evie had to admit she preferred. She felt comforted, as if he could keep her safe and handle anything she didn't want to. She liked the feeling of femininity she felt around him. She had hidden from it for a long time, and now she wanted to feel like that near him.

She locked the door then King took her arm, leading her down the sidewalk to his car and opening the door for her. After she'd slid inside the front seat, he closed her door then walked around the car to get behind the driver's wheel.

"That a first for you?"

King laughed. "Are you implying I'm missing Henry?"

"Are you?"

"Yes, but not for the work. We've spent many hours together over the years, so it's like my left arm is missing."

"It's going to be an adjustment for you."

"For Henry, too. He's already called to check on me six times."

"I'll have to call him and tell him I'll keep an eye on you."

"Are you trying to relieve him or make him worry more?"

Evie laughed. "Both."

King pulled into the parking lot of the Pink Slipper.

"In the space of five minutes, you can drive from one end of Treepoint to the other unless you get caught by the only red light in town."

"It is small. That's why the Pink Slipper is so busy tonight; it's the only restaurant in town with a liquor license," she told him when he couldn't find a parking space in the crowded lot.

"So far," King said, getting out of the car. Evie gave him a startled look when he opened her door. He took her hand, helping her out of the car. "I'm thinking of giving them some competition."

"I thought you were retiring?"

"I have no plans to open a strip club, if that's what you're thinking. I'm thinking of something like this, a restaurant with a bar."

"That's good because your chances of opening a strip club in Treepoint are nil. I don't even believe some of these people get naked when they have sex." Evie's voice had dropped to a whisper as they entered the club.

"Oh, I think they do," King said, staring around the busy restaurant.

"I don't know," Evie continued to tease him as the hostess showed them to an intimate table.

Once seated, Evie stared across at King, admiring his harsh, good looks while the waitress took their drink order.

"When did you start drinking wine again?"

Evie looked down at her hands, adjusting her utensils. "I'm trying to cut back on the hard liquor. I'm not getting any younger. Did you know excessive drinking can age you?"

King took a drink of whiskey, his amused expression gentle. "You look beautiful. You don't look a day over twenty-one."

"Liar." She rolled her eyes at his transparent compliment.

The waitress took their dinner order at that moment. Once she'd left, Evie watched King enviously as she took a sip of her wine, wincing at the taste just as his eyes sharpened at something over her shoulder. She was about to turn when a familiar voice greeted them. While Evie's stomach lurched as she gazed up into her sister's face, Merrick came to his wife's side, sliding his arm protectively around her waist. Evie's lips tightened, her hand clenching the wine glass, threatening to snap the fragile stem.

"Evie."

"Pastor Patterson." Evie refused to acknowledge her sister.

"I haven't seen you in church since I've gotten here. Lucky said you were a faithful parishioner when he was pastor."

Evie decided to be truthful. "I've decided to go to the church in Jamestown." She almost regretted her bluntness when she saw the hurt look on Merrick's face. He was a nice man--too nice--and he was completely blind to his wife's faults.

"I'm sorry to hear that. I was hoping you and Brooke would overcome your childhood arguments now that you are older. Brooke has sent numerous invitations for dinner; the least you could do is respond. Evie, it is your niece that she is carrying. We really would like our baby to get to know her mother's twin."

Evie ignored King's body tensing across the table at Merrick's cutting words.

"I don't think that's going to be possible, Pastor. I'm afraid I haven't reached the point of turning the other cheek."

"Evie, that was uncalled for." Brooke's tearful voice drew both men's eyes, one more discerning than the other.

"I see I was wrong in trying to make an effort to encourage Brooke to make an attempt of reconciliation. I hope your new church can give you what you need."

"I hope you take those blinders off, Merrick. I truly wish you the best." Evie was sincere; she wouldn't wish Brooke on her worst enemy, much less a man like Merrick who deserved better.

"Let's go, darling. I told you it was useless." Brooke gave King a sweet smile before turning into her husband's protective arm as he led her away from the table.

"The check I had done on her doesn't do her justice. The poor bastard."

"Why did you run a check on her?" Evie made herself lower her voice.

"Don't be angry, but I had you checked out, too."

Evie started to smart off then closed her mouth. "We had you checked out, too, but you knew that, just as I should have. So, you already knew my past before I told you?"

"Some of it, yes, but I became curious after you told me what happened. It didn't match the report I was given, so I looked into it further. That's when I discovered one of the men's testimonies about Brooke's involvement."

"You already knew about Levi before I told you?"

King nodded his head.

"You want to know the ironic part? She did it to break up my friendship with Shade, and it only strengthened it. She was angry we were stationed together. I wouldn't have made it through those days after Levi was killed if I hadn't had him to lean on."

"I'm glad he was there for you." Evie saw the truth in his eyes.

"She has the life I wanted. Levi and I were going to get married and make a family together. She never wanted kids, though. She hated them."

"Evie…"

At that moment, the waitress brought their food, and thankfully, the topic was changed, but the lighthearted atmosphere was gone. Evie managed to take a couple of bites yet couldn't force herself to take another drink of the appalling wine.

King motioned for the waitress to bring the ticket, giving her his credit card.

"Finish eating. I'll be fine in a minute."

"Yours isn't the only appetite she ruined," he said, signing the check and rising to his feet.

They drove back to her house in silence. "King, I..." she started when they got to her door.

"I'll see you tomorrow, Evie." His mouth brushed her lips before he stepped back, going to his car. He waited until she was inside before pulling out of her driveway. She had been tempted to invite him in but had not wanted to return to her habit of using sex to escape the pain of her past.

Evie went into the living room, sitting down on the couch and staring into space.

King had irrevocably changed her; all she could think of was wanting him. She had missed him and wanted to touch him. None of that had to do with missing Levi. She was tired and aggravated at Brooke, but she didn't feel like sitting and thinking about the past; it had finally lost its grim hold on her.

Evie got off the couch and went to bed.

* * *

Monday's were always busy days. She was returning a file to the office when she looked out into the lobby to see Beth sitting there. Evie opened the door, motioning her back.

"I didn't know you had an appointment today with Dr. Jones." She caught the brief twinge of pain Beth tried to hide.

"I didn't. I haven't been feeling well, so I thought I would get Dr. Jones to check me out. I know I'm probably just being paranoid, though."

"I have a room available. Go on inside, and I'll tell the doctor you're here." Evie went to the nurse and passed along the message.

Beth was carrying twins, and while she had a naturally-fair complexion, she seemed pale to Evie. She went into the exam room she had placed Beth in, going to the cabinet.

"I'm going to get some blood work on you, Beth, while we wait for the doctor."

"Okay." As her friend's worried gaze caught hers, Evie swallowed, forcing herself to focus. She had been trained to maintain a profession demeanor, yet Beth had become a close friend. She had become more of a sister to her than her own twin.

When Dr. Jones came in, her eyes showed the same concern as Evie's. Both women worked together to check Beth out then talked silently outside before going back in to Beth.

"Beth, I'm putting you on bed rest."

"Before you freak out," Evie started, "I'll take over your patients for the rest of the week. Besides, you're already training Dayton to take over for you while you're on maternity leave anyway."

"All right. I want to say no, but I'm not going to take any chances with the babies."

"Good choice. Your blood pressure is slightly elevated, so I want you to get plenty of sleep and relaxation. No worrying over those clients, either," Dr. Jones ordered in her no-nonsense voice.

"If Evie is watching over them, then I know they'll be in good hands."

"Did you drive yourself in?" Evie asked her suspiciously.

"Yes, I didn't want to worry Razer," Beth admitted.

Evie slid out her phone.

"You wouldn't dare," Beth said, reaching out to try to take the phone away.

Evie pressed Razer's number, putting the phone to her ear. When he came on the line, she explained where Beth was and the doctor's orders. She hung up after a brief word from him.

"Traitor."

Evie shrugged unconcerned. "He would have kicked my ass if he found out you were here and I didn't tell him."

"Now he's going to kick mine," Beth said, feeling sorry for herself. Evie recognized the emotional signs of Beth's advanced pregnancy.

"That man would never hurt one of those blonde hairs of yours," Evie said unsympathetically.

"I'm going to pay you back for this one day," she threatened.

"Maybe so, but you're a hell of a lot easier to face than Razer."

Chapter Twenty-five

King stood in the parking lot of the church, waiting for Evie to drop off the clothing she had collected for the store. The backyard of the church was filled with the town celebrating the Fourth of July, so King's eyes traveled over the yard, looking for his daughter.

She was leaning against one of the large oak trees as she waited for Shade to finish his conversation with Viper and Rider. Shade was facing his wife while the other two men had their backs to her.

If he hadn't been watching, he would have missed the silent communication between the couple. Lily was staring at Shade with a soft smile on her face, and for a flash of a second, her face turned to one of heated desire before she blushed, regaining her composure. Shade caught the look and returned it with one of his own. Excusing himself from his friends, he stalked across the yard to his wife who was frantically looking around to make sure no one was watching. Her husband captured her, bending down to whisper something in her ear before placing an arm around her shoulder then maneuvering her through the crowd.

"Are you spying on them?" Evie's amused voice drew his attention.

"Shade really loves her, doesn't he?" It wasn't a question.

"That's what I've been telling you for the last six months."

They opened the gate to the backyard as Shade and Lily were about to reach it.

"Leaving early?" King watched as Lily turned a bright red.

"The heat is getting to Lily. We thought we would go home until it cools down then come back for the fireworks," Shade explained with an impassive face.

King smiled down at his embarrassed daughter. "I'll see you later tonight then."

"You two have fun," Lily said quickly as Shade led her to his bike.

King stared after them as Shade drove off.

"They are still considered newlyweds," Evie laughed.

"I never thought I would see the day where she was that happy." His voice was thick with emotion as he turned back to Evie. "I'm glad we came."

"Me, too. I haven't missed this picnic since I've come to Treepoint, but I don't know if I would have come if Lily hadn't told me Brooke wouldn't be here today." Lily had told her Brooke had taken her new niece back to Georgia for their mother to see and would be gone the next three weeks. Evie was hurt her mother and Brooke were so close while their mother had turned her back on her; Evie couldn't imagine turning her back on one of her own children.

As they filled their plates at the many tables that had been set up, King was much more wary this time about the food; he only dumped small amounts onto his plate.

"You're learning."

"I learn from my mistakes," King said, following Evie to where The Last Riders were seated at a picnic table.

He hadn't met them yet, but he recognized them from their pictures that had been given to him when he'd had Shade checked out. They were a hard group of men that had faced many challenges. King had grown up rough, but a couple of them could probably teach him a lesson or two.

"Hell no, why didn't someone warn me they would be here," the one King recognized as Train groaned.

King looked in the direction he was staring at in horror.

The group of women entering the picnic were dressed flashy, to say the least. One with bright red hair was dressed seductively in a wrap dress that left her chest mostly bare. She had tattoos on her chest, which he couldn't make out from the distance, and she was pushing a double stroller like it was a weapon of mass destruction, sending people scurrying out of their path. If he were to imagine what hard-living biker women looked like, these women would fit that picture in his mind. They were dressed in leather, boasted tats and had hair that went the gamut of colors. One of the women was taller and leaner than the rest, wearing tight, black jeans and a t-shirt with metal spikes on the shoulders. Her cold gaze surveyed the picnic guests before moving to stand behind the young girls.

The women were heading toward their table.

"Shit."

"Calm down, Train. We'll protect you." Lucky laughed at his friend's predicament.

"I don't know what the fuck you think is so funny; you're not a pastor anymore. They're going to consider you fresh meat," Train taunted.

"Hey, bitch, where have you been?" King stiffened next to Evie when he realized one of the women was addressing her. Her hand quickly lay on his thigh to prevent him from snapping a reply to her rude greeting.

The woman in the wrap dress smacked the other woman on the arm. "What did I tell you about your fucking mouth?" She then turned to look down at Evie. "You going to introduce us to your new man?"

"King, this is Sex Piston. The one with the metal spikes is Killyama. The one with the purple hair is Crazy Bitch. And T.A. and Fat Louise are over there with the little girls, breaking the line to get their faces painted."

"Got to teach kids to take up for themselves." Sex Piston bragged.

"They're the ones breaking the line." King watched the woman shrug unconcernedly, never taking her shrewd gaze off him.

Out of the corner of his eye, he saw Train try to talk to the one with spikes; however, she ignored him, walking to Lucky. "This seat taken?"

"Bliss was just getting us—no, have a seat." Lucky scooted over, letting the abrasive woman sit down. King then noticed a small, attractive blonde turn on her heel, going to another picnic table. Evie just shook her head at him when he asked why the woman didn't return to the table. Within seconds, King had his answer as the table was completely taken over by the crew of women.

Not long after they sat down, King was taking a drink of his iced tea when Sex Piston's baby began crying. She picked the infant up, and without showing even a hint of embarrassment, she pulled her dress to the side, unsnapping a flap before letting the baby nurse in front of God and everyone at the picnic.

"One of nature's most beautiful moments, isn't it?" Killyama said.

"That's easy for you to say; he isn't chewing your nipple off." Sex Piston replied sarcastically.

King choked, trying to blink back the painful tears in his eyes.

"They have that effect on everyone," Train said grimly.

"I see Willa decided to come after all. I'm going to go say hello." Evie jumped up, glad to take the opportunity for escape.

King grabbed Evie's hand. "I'll come with you," he said, hurriedly getting to his feet.

"Coward," Evie remarked when they were away from the picnic table.

"What are they?"

"They belong to the Destructors."

"Another motorcycle club?"

"Yes."

"And I thought Treepoint was a sleepy, little town," King muttered snidely.

"Technically, the Destructors live in Jamestown, but Sex Piston likes to visit, a lot."

"Sweet Jesus."

"Hi, Willa."

"Evie, King."

"Did you bring dessert?" King asked, smiling down at the pretty woman. She was as short as the other blonde, but while the other was slim and perky, Willa was heavier and more reserved. There was no comparison to King when he looked into her cornflower blue eyes.

"Yes, I brought the cupcakes with the sparklers." King started to go to the table to get one but saw the table surrounded by children.

"Sorry." When Willa laughed at his show of disappointment, King's mouth almost dropped open, staring at the woman in surprise. When she forgot to be shy, her face lit up, her smile showing twin dimples. A sharp pinch on his arm had him looking at Evie.

"Be polite," she hissed. King could see his staring was giving Willa the wrong impression, but he hadn't worked with women most of his life without knowing how to handle them.

"I'm sorry I was staring, Willa, but it's just so refreshing to see a stunning woman with such natural beauty."

As Willa turned bright red, King thought she would high-tail it away, but instead, she began asking him questions about Queen City.

"What did you do there?"

"I ran several businesses," he responded gently.

"That sounds interesting. I get tempted every so often to open a bakery, but I really don't want to be tied down to working in one every day. I already have enough to keep me busy."

"I may have a solution. Now that I'm living here, I'm thinking of opening a restaurant with a bar, and I would certainly be willing to buy your desserts for our menu on a regular basis."

"I would like that. I could create a few things just for your menu."

They continued to talk until King noticed Willa turned pale when a large man came into the picnic yard with a group of five children. He noticed her hands shake as she tucked her hair behind her ear. Even Evie noticed her behavior, giving King a concerned glance.

As the group grew closer, King saw the man look over at them. He had a pleasant face, but the look in his eyes told King he was presenting a façade. He was proved correct when he saw Willa and moved toward their group.

"Hello, Evie, Willa." He nodded his head genially in King's direction, yet he didn't take his eyes off Willa. "I thought you said you weren't coming to the picnic. You had a big order due; that was why you couldn't come with me."

"I did—I do." Willa's voice shook. "I was just delivering one of the orders here. I stopped to say hello to Evie and King before I left to make the other deliveries."

"Oh." The man's accusing eyes didn't soften.

"Lewis is an employee at the factory." At Evie's introduction, King extended his hand to him, which Lewis shook before turning his attention immediately back to Willa who was trying to unobtrusively leave.

"You're a lucky man to have so many children. You and your wife must be very proud."

Lewis's mouth tightened. "They aren't all mine; two are

my sister's."

Evie looked up at King, explaining, "His sister used to be an employee of ours before she died."

"I'm sorry to hear that," King offered his condolences.

Lewis shrugged, turning once again back to Willa, stepping closer to her. "You going to come back after you make the deliveries?"

"No, I need to get started on the orders for tomorrow," Willa said, taking a step backward.

"Willa, be careful," King tried to warn her, but the jumpy woman was trying to get away from Lewis and wasn't paying attention to where she was backing up. She collided with Lucky who was carrying a large plate of the cupcakes, mashing them into his chest. When he tried to catch himself, he took a half step backward, bumping into Rider, who dropped his plate onto the ground.

"What the fuck, Lucky? Watch what you're doing!" Rider said. King put out his hand to steady Willa, helping her to regain her balance.

"I'm so sorry." Willa took the plate of cupcakes away from Lucky.

"You always were clumsy," Lewis said, taking the plate of cupcakes away from Willa and thrusting them toward King, who automatically reached out to take the plate.

"Here, let me." Evie took the plate instead, stepping to the side and setting it down on the table before grabbing a handful of napkins.

One of the children with Lewis bent down to pick up one of the cupcakes Rider had dropped and began eating it.

"No, Chrissy. That's dirty." Willa tried to take the cupcake away, but the little girl shoved her hand, making her hit Rider in the balls. Willa jerked her hand away as if it had been scalded.

"Chrissy, put that cupcake down right now!" Lewis yelled.

The little girl started wailing, throwing the cupcake at

her father who dodged it, so it hit Willa instead.

When Willa's bottom lip began to tremble, King grabbed her, pulling her to his side, laughing. "I told you everyone would be fighting for your desserts."

Chapter Twenty-six

Evie closed the door to her house behind them. "I think I have cupcake in my hair," she said, giggling as she stared at King.

"You have no reason to complain. I have to get a shower. I feel like I'm covered in chocolate."

"You are. Come on; let's go take a shower."

King hesitated. "You sure?"

Evie stopped on the bottom step. "It was really sweet what you did for Willa. I didn't know you could be sweet."

"Did it give me brownie points with you?"

"Absolutely." Evie grinned, holding out her hand to him.

They continued up the steps to her bedroom. She had decorated Beth's old room in peaches and greens, going for a calming oasis and succeeding in making herself one. They took their clothes off, careful to bundle them up so the cupcake crumbs wouldn't fall onto her new carpet.

"I'll throw them in the washer in the morning," she told King as he started the shower, pulling Evie in with him. "Ugh. This is an old house; it takes time for the water to warm up." She hated cold showers.

Once the water had finally warmed and they were able

to wash off the sticky chocolate, King's shoulders started shaking with laughter.

"What?" Evie asked.

"Did you see Rider's face when she hit his dick?"

"Willa's was worse." Evie started laughing. "Lucky looked like he was going to cry over those cupcakes, too." She laid her head on the shower wall. "It's not funny; I thought Willa was going to cry. And Lewis was so jealous, he was about to have a stroke. I don't think she likes him, though."

"You think? When she tried to go to her car, he and all five kids followed." King put his hand on the shower wall as their merriment filled the room.

"Did you see how mad Lucky was? When he tried to get Lewis to back off, one of those kids actually kicked him." Evie was laughing so hard she was hiccupping.

A serious expression crossed King's face. "I think he's been harassing her from the way she acted."

Evie nodded her head in agreement. "I'll stop by her house my next day off and see what's going on."

"Good idea. Something tells me it's not a good situation."

"Me, either." The gravity of Willa's situation enabled Evie to regain control.

"I missed you, King. Somehow, when I'm around you, I feel like laughing again." She rinsed out her hair then, reaching out, pulled him under the showerhead with her. "I don't want to be lonely anymore," she admitted.

"God, Evie. You think you've been lonely?" He tugged her out of the shower, drying her off carefully before rubbing the towel roughly over his own body. He then picked her up and carried her into the bedroom. Sitting down on the bed, he placed her on his lap. "For the last thirty years, I've spent my life not becoming close to anyone. I even gave my daughter up, thinking I was protecting her. It was myself I was trying to protect, though; I didn't want to lose someone again after losing my sister. Instead of straightening my life out, I hid in a life that wasn't worth living. I have a lot of sins to atone for."

His tortured eyes made Evie want to cry. She reached out, cupping his cheek. "No one could hurt us worse than what we've done to ourselves."

"When you left, a part of me left with you. I thought that drive back to Queen City, leaving Lily behind, was painful; but when you left, you took my soul with you. I'm never going to let you leave me again."

"I don't think you're going to have to worry about that because I'm not going anywhere." When she leaned upward to kiss his mouth, her tongue licked his bottom lip then tugged it until he opened to her. Her hands went to his shoulders, pressing him backwards onto the bed. She placed her legs on each side of his hips, sitting on his stomach, bending down to explore his mouth.

Evie raised her head to catch her breath, and King said, "Did anyone ever tell you you're an exceptional kisser?"

"A time or two." Evie rose up on one hand, reaching back with the other to place his cock at her opening. Wiggling her hips, she let the tip of his dick barely enter her. Her hand then went down between her thighs, rubbing her clit.

"Would you like me to do that?" King brought his knees up and Evie leaned backwards, placing her weight on them.

"That's okay. I've got this," she moaned, letting another inch of him slide inside her.

King arched under her, driving himself fully inside her.

"That wasn't fair. I wanted to go slow."

"I didn't." As his hands gripped her hips, sliding her up and down his cock, Evie was surprised he was able to lift her weight. Correctly reading her surprise, he said, "I work out."

"Yes, you do," she moaned, rubbing her clit harder and thrusting herself down on him.

King arched, groaning, and then stopped moving.

"Evie, is that a stripper pole by your closet?"

"Yes."

"Why is there a stripper pole in your bedroom?"

"Because I use it to exercise," she said, becoming frustrated. "King, when I said you didn't need to do anything, I was just joking!"

"Are you going to give me a show later on?"

Evie stopped moving, looking down at him. "That depends on whether you keep me hanging much longer," she snapped.

King tossed her to her back, surging inside her in a hard thrust that tore a scream from her throat. "Baby, I'm going to make you so happy, when you dance on that pole you'll feel like you're flying."

I feel pretty damn good now, Evie thought. Her thighs gripped his hips as he fucked her. Evie was used to a variety of men and sexual positions; none of them felt as intimate as King making love to her.

Evie felt her body building toward a climax, gripping him tighter.

"Come with me, Evie." As his command sent her over, she felt his cock come deep within her.

As soon as he rolled off her, she ran into the bathroom, slamming the bathroom door.

"Evie, what's wrong?" She heard him but didn't answer. Grabbing a wash cloth, knowing it would be useless, she still had to try.

She frantically began washing herself, rubbing between her legs so hard she was becoming red and raw.

"What in the hell are you doing?" He jerked the wet cloth from her, tossing it into the sink.

Evie burst into tears, burying her face into her hands. "Don't hate me. I was supposed to go on another form of birth control. I made my appointment with my OB-GYN, but with Beth on bed rest, I didn't have time."

"Evie, baby, calm down. It's all right."

"You hated Brenda for getting pregnant."

King closed the toilet lid, sitting down. His hands pulled her between his legs then his mouth kissed her bare belly. "Evie, there is no comparison between you and Brenda. I was high and don't even remember fucking her; I wouldn't have touched her with a ten-foot pole otherwise. The bitch never even told me she was pregnant. She kept Lily hidden from me because the woman knew I would be furious."

The day he had seen Lily sitting outside that apartment building, dirty and underfed, was the worst day of his life. That he hadn't known of her existence hadn't eased his conscience; it had made him ache at the time he had lost with Lily. Her being born, her first step, her first word. To see the little girl run to him yelling Daddy when he came home from work. The bonding of a father to a daughter. That time couldn't be recaptured. He hated Brenda. There was no comparison between her and Evie.

"To be honest, I wouldn't mind if you became pregnant. I missed raising Lily and would really like a do-over at it. So, if you do get pregnant, I promise I won't suck as bad at it the second time around." The thought of holding a child they had created filled an empty hole he hadn't even been aware existed. This would be a love he could make himself worthy of earning this time.

"Really?" Evie raised her face from her hands.

"Really." His violet eyes were filled with agony. "Do you know Lily's only called me Dad when she thought she or I was going to die?"

"King, you haven't been the perfect father, but it's not too late. I've known Lily a long time; it won't be the last time she calls you Dad. Knowing her, she wants to make sure it's okay with you. Talk to her."

"I don't know how I ever created something as beautiful as her."

"Baby, you didn't do it alone."

"Brenda doesn't deserve any credit for giving birth to Lily."

"I wasn't talking about Lily." Evie looked down into the face that looked so much like his daughter. "Lily told Shade that, if things hadn't turned out the way they had, she wouldn't have ended up in Kentucky. I don't believe that, but I do believe she ended up exactly where she belongs. Just like you, King. Maybe you weren't a good father to her when she was a child, but you have the rest of your life to make it up to her. Talk to her and clear the air. Lily's not the only one who needs to heal."

"I don't want to bring up the past and upset her."

"Then don't. Talk about the future, and let her know you're always going to be there for her. She's come so far over the last six months, and once she knows you're not against her marriage anymore, she won't feel torn between the two of you."

King stood, taking her in his arms. "Let's get some sleep."

"No stripper pole tonight?"

"Tonight, I'm going to be the one to please you. I have a lot to live up to. It's hard for one man to live up to so much competition."

King packed her back to the bedroom, laying her down on the bed.

Evie searched his eyes, looking for censure or jealously, and found none. "King…"

"Evie, I have never been afraid of a little competition." His fingers twisted her nipple. "I'm certainly willing to prove I can keep you satisfied."

Evie grinned back. "King, you can prove yourself to me all night long."

* * *

Evie set her orange juice down on the table, staring at King in shock. "You're going to do what?"

"Don't look so shocked," King grumbled. "Shade invited me to go on the fishing trip with all the men the night you have Beth's shower, and I accepted."

"You've never went fishing or camped out a night in

196

your life."

King shrugged. "How hard could it be?"

Evie spread some jam on her toast. "The only reason they are going to get out of attending the baby shower is Lily scarred them for life with Sex Piston's."

"All of The Last Riders are going, so I take it as a good sign they invited me."

"Bullshit. You just don't want to be stuck with all the women by yourself."

"That's not true," King denied, pouring himself a cup of coffee. He had come to the conclusion that building a relationship with Lily was more important than breaking her marriage to Shade. He still didn't trust the man, but he was certain he would never hurt Lily. He figured going on the camping trip with Shade would show Lily he was willing to try. Shade had looked surprised he had accepted the invitation King was certain had been given after Lily's prompting.

"You do know you'll have to shit in the woods?"

"Are Sex Piston and her crew coming to the shower?"

"Yes."

"Then camping will be a new experience I will thoroughly enjoy."

"Sure it will," Evie said doubtfully.

"I'm beginning to feel insulted." King looked at her over the real-estate section of the newspaper.

Evie eyed King's immaculate clothes. "When I look at you, 'outdoorsman' doesn't come to mind."

King sighed and changed the subject. "I have a meeting this morning with the owner of the property I told you about that I want to buy for the restaurant."

"I can fucking guarantee he won't be wearing a two-thousand-dollar suit."

"It's all about intimidation to get the best price for the property," King informed her.

Evie took a bite of her toast, chewing it thoughtfully. "Have you met Drake Hall yet?"

"No, the realtor set the appointment up for me."

"He's not going to be intimidated by you. You want a better price on the property, take Bliss with you; he'll be too busy staring at her tits to concentrate on you chewing his price down."

"I think I can handle him. I've bought over a hundred properties in Queen City."

Evie finished her toast, placing her plate in the sink. "Don't say I didn't warn you." She went back to the table, bending down to give him a kiss. "I have to go. I need to see a couple of Beth's patients before I go to the grocery store to buy the groceries for tonight's party."

"You need me to do anything before I leave? Shade and Rider aren't picking me up until this afternoon."

"You could blow the balloons up for me. They're on the table in the living room." Evie could tell from his face he was less than thrilled by the challenge of blowing the balloons up.

"I meant errands you needed done." He clarified.

"Nope, just the balloons. I think if Shade could make another masterpiece out of diapers, then you can blow up a few balloons."

Chapter Twenty-seven

"So, what's it like going from a whole clubhouse of men fucking you to just one man?"

Evie stared at Killyama as she refilled her tea glass, tempted to dump the whole pitcher on her head.

"Killyama!" Beth reproved her friend, saving Evie from having to answer her question in front of a whole roomful of women, one being the daughter of the man she was in love with.

"Shit, it's not like everyone else isn't thinking the same thing," Killyama continued.

Evie avoided Lily's amused gaze as she sat down on the couch beside Beth.

"Well?"

Evie was trying to remind herself the woman was a good friend of Beth's and that was why she had invited her and Sex Piston's crew. However, she was seriously thinking of shoving one of the many pacifiers Beth had received as gifts down her freaking throat. The woman wasn't going to shut up until she answered, though.

"I'm in love with him." *Where in the hell did that come from?* Evie had never had any intention of stating it so bluntly, but the bitch hadn't let up since she had let them in her door.

The room went silent, which wasn't an easy thing with so many women packed into the small house. All eyes shifted to Lily, waiting for her reaction.

She got up from the chair she was sitting at. "I know you hate hugs, but I'm going to give you one anyway." Evie opened her arms and Lily bent down, giving her a hug that brought tears to her eyes.

"Fuck, if I'd know we were going to turn into a bunch of crying pussies, I would have kept my mouth shut," Killyama griped.

Evie and Lily broke apart, laughing.

"That would have been asking for the impossible," Beth threatened her friend with a heated glare.

Evie gave Beth a reassuring smile that she wasn't upset, picking up the bowl of chips and passing them around like nothing had been said. She was determined to make a success of her party, despite her guests. She had promised Razer that Beth would have a good time after he had packed his wife in earlier, placing her on the couch. He hadn't wanted to leave her, despite the men impatiently blowing their horns from outside, until Evie had promised to take good care of her until his pickup of her tomorrow. Both Beth and Lily were spending the night with her, and Evie was looking forward to the girl time.

Evie passed the chips to Willa.

"No, thanks."

"Motherfucker. What is this?" Crazy Bitch asked.

"Peanut butter candy," Willa answered.

"My freaking God," Jewell moaned. "This is better than sex with Lucky, and if you tell him, I'll deny it," she threatened.

The women turned to look at Beth.

"How would I know? The extent of my knowledge about Lucky is kissing." She shrugged, blushing. "We stopped seeing each other before it progressed that far."

Evie noticed Willa pick up the bowl of chips. Thinking

the casual talk about sex was upsetting her, Evie sought to change the subject.

"It's really delicious, Willa. Could you show me how to make it?"

"What about you, Evie? Which is better, the candy or Dean?" Killyama butted in before Willa could answer. She recognized the crushed look on Willa's face. Evie wondered if Knox would arrest her if she killed the bitch.

Fed up, Evie put her hands on her hips, glaring at the interested women, who were avoiding Willa munching on chips, and Lily's embarrassed expression.

"I am only going to say this once, then we're changing the subject. There are two brothers I never did. One is Shade, the other is Lucky. Now, the candy is freaking awesome, and if you want to compare it to something, then it's better than Winter's lasagna."

"It can't be that good," Bliss said, getting up from her chair to get a piece of the candy. The women burst out laughing at her expression. "I'm your new best friend," Bliss stated, picking up another piece before turning to sit back down. "That stuff is addictive."

"It's my best seller. I can't make it fast enough," Willa explained with a shy smile.

"I'm going to take some back to the clubhouse, if you don't mind. Rider loves peanut butter. I've been trying to get him to fix the garbage disposal for a month, and that stuff will give me the bribe I need," Bliss stated around a mouthful of candy.

Sex Piston reached over to take a piece of the dwindling candy. "Girl, you could get any man in town with that stuff."

"I'd do her for it," Jewell said, reaching for another, but Bliss got up, moving the tray to the kitchen.

Willa turned so red Evie almost laughed, but she didn't want to draw even more attention to the embarrassed woman.

"The only men who want me are the ones who think

I'll be their slave in the kitchen."

"I'm sure that's not true," Lily said, reaching out to take her friend's hand.

Willa made a face. "Believe me, it is. When I get asked out on a date, they never take me out to a restaurant; they expect me to cook for them."

"Lewis one of those men?" Evie questioned, watching Willa's reaction.

"Lewis thinks I would make a good replacement for the wife that ran away with another man." Willa's face was white and her eyes held fear that turned Evie's stomach. "Now that he's raising his sister's kids with his own three, he thinks I would make the perfect mother. He says I'm too fat and ugly for other men to chase, and I can cook, clean and babysit. Of course, the most important part is I have a thriving business to sponge from."

"You need me to have a talk with this fucker?" Killyama asked, sitting down next to Willa.

Willa's eyes opened wide at Killyama's blunt words. "That's okay. I've got it under control." Evie didn't believe her; she would have a talk with Shade when he came back tomorrow.

While Beth continued opening her presents, Evie organized all of them so Razer wouldn't have any difficulty loading them up tomorrow when he picked her up.

"Who is this one from?" Beth asked when Lily handed her the last one. "It's from Pastor Patterson's wife. He gave it to me today. He told me Brooke had left it before she had gone to visit her mother."

"Did she know we were having a shower for Beth?"

"Yes, she called the store today to ask if I could see the pastor had dinner tonight. I told her I couldn't because I would be too busy helping you with the shower. Rachel volunteered to fix him something before she left, though," Lily said, picking up the discarded wrapping paper.

"I fixed him a bowl of soup. That man is helpless in the kitchen," Rachel said, taking a handful of chips. "She even had the nerve to ask me if I thought Lily would come in the morning to fix him breakfast. I told her no, that she was spending the night with you and Beth. The man can fix his own bowl of cereal. If my three brothers can manage to feed themselves, then I think the pastor can, too."

"Your brothers can't cook?" Evie joked.

"No, they think that's what I'm for. I keep hoping at least one of them will get married off." She stared at Killyama. "You dating anyone?"

"No."

"Want me to fix you up with one of them?" Rachel asked hopefully.

"Which one?"

"Any one you want." Evie couldn't smother her laughter at Rachel's eagerness.

Killyama looked at Rachel suspiciously. "Which one has the most guns?"

"Tate."

"Hook me up. I'll give him a try first."

"First?" Rachel lost her smile.

Killyama nodded. "I'll give all three a try before I make my mind up."

"Never mind," Rachel told her. "They already fight at the drop of a hat; I don't need them killing each other over a woman."

"If you change your mind, let me know."

Without a word, Rachel got up, going into the kitchen to try to get another piece of candy from the tray Bliss was guarding.

It was after midnight before the women began leaving. Holding the door open as they left, Evie heard the rumbling of thunder.

"I didn't know a storm was moving in," Evie remarked, seeing the lightning flash across the sky.

"I didn't, either." Winter paused in the threshold. "Will the men be all right?"

"Yes. It's not like they're sleeping in tents. Cash's cabin is big enough to hold them all," Evie assured her.

"That's good. I would have worried about them."

"They're perfectly safe. They have all the amenities: a television, radio and weed. I'm sure they're just fine."

After everyone left, Evie and Lily cleaned up the mess. When Beth would have gotten up to help, Evie threatened to call Razer, so Beth sank back against the couch, wincing.

"Are you all right?" Evie asked.

"I'm fine. Just a little indigestion. I shouldn't have eaten all those meatballs."

"Me, either," Evie agreed.

With most of the clean-up finished, they decided to turn in. Evie carried Beth several pillows and a blanket. Lily would sleep in her old bedroom upstairs, which Evie had converted into a spare bedroom.

"Comfortable?"

"Are you kidding me? It's summer, yet you'd think it was winter outside."

"I was afraid you would get cold with the air conditioning," she explained.

"It feels fine in here. This couch is as big as a twin bed, and the bathroom is just right there. Go to bed."

"I'm going. You got your cell phone?" Beth picked it up from the coffee table, waving it in the air.

"Goodnight," Evie said, going to the steps.

"Night."

"Are you sure you don't want me to stay down here with you until you feel better?" Lily hesitated by her sister's side.

"Go to bed, Lily."

"I'm going."

As both women went up the stairs together, Evie noticed Lily looked tense. "I'll check on her in the middle of the night," Evie said before going in her room.

"I will, too. I don't sleep very well in storms." The loud

thunder at that second made both women jump.

"I don't, either." She went in her room after making sure Lily didn't need anything, changing into her nightgown. The sound of the pouring rain was hitting the window when Evie climbed into bed, hoping the storm wouldn't last long.

* * *

King lit his cigar while sitting in the boat. They had been out on the water for over an hour. Shade and Rider both had their fishing lines in the water.

"We could go back to shore and get you another pole," Rider offered.

"No, thanks. I would probably lose that one, too," King stated, biting down on his cigar in aggravation. He was never going to hear the end of it from Evie when she found out he had battled a fish and the fish had won, taking his fishing pole with him. He was contemplating the believability of telling her a lake monster was hidden in the depths of the small lake but didn't believe she would buy it.

"Don't feel bad. We've all lost poles. Of course, we were all drunk as shit at the time," Rider joked.

King looked at a silent Shade, who sat staring into the lake. He was going to have to make the first move to repair the damage he had created.

"How's Lily adapting to the new minister and his wife?" King decided to start the conversation with a neutral topic.

"She's adjusting, but there's not a connection with Merrick like Lucky."

"Dean's living at the clubhouse now?" King broached the subject he was most interested in.

"Yes." Shade's answer was short and told him nothing.

"How's that working out?"

When Shade sighed, turning to look at him, Rider had a smile on his face as he listened. King was aware he was making an ass out of himself without the man making it obvious.

"If you want to know if he participates in the club's activities, yes, he does. Not that it's any business of yours. Lily and I have our own separate house. Neither of us want Lily to see him when he's partying, so I text him when Lily's in the house. Dean cares about Lily and has no desire to tarnish his image to her."

"That's a lot of work for you two to make sure Lily isn't uncomfortable."

"She's worth the trouble." Shade's words brought a sharp pain to King's chest. He had never gone to the trouble of making Lily happy one time while he had condemned Shade for being an unemotional bastard.

"Yes, she is. Now that I'm in town, I want to get to know her better." King hesitated before adding, "Both of you. I don't want to invade your lives, just become a small part of it. I want to be able to have a relationship with my grandchildren when you two have a child." It was the closest he could come to telling Shade he was accepting their marriage, regardless of whether he gave a damn or not. The only opinion Shade cared about was Lily's. King agreed his opinion didn't count, but he didn't want any hard feelings to linger over the years ahead of them.

The boat went silent; the only sound was the water lapping against the side.

"Got another cigar?" Shade eventually asked. It was the closest thing to an olive branch as King was going to get.

"Yes, I do." King pulled his stash out of his tackle box, offering one to each man. As Shade and Rider each took one, going back to their fishing, King relaxed on his seat while the men talked, the atmosphere lightening. Shade actually spoke to him several times without him initiating the conversation. It wasn't much, but it was the start to a new beginning.

Shade and Rider both managed to catch six fish before the sky darkened and they decided to go back to camp. They docked the boat, carrying their tackle boxes and poles as they walked to the cabin. The others had fished from shore and had already begun frying their catches.

"Where's your pole?" Viper asked from the grill.

"He lost it," Rider volunteered the information.

The Last Riders broke into laughter, making jokes at his expense. King took it good-naturedly but promised himself he would show no mercy if the shoe was ever on the other foot.

When Viper and Cash served up the fish, which was surprisingly good, King determined it was worth the ribbing he had taken. After dinner, they all pitched in to clean up outside then went inside to get away from the insects and play some cards.

He was winning his fourth hand in a row when he looked up to see Shade was no longer seated at the table.

"What are you doing?" King asked his son-in-law when he saw him gathering his things.

"I'm going back."

"Why?" King looked down at his watch. "It's after midnight."

"I know what time it is. The storm is getting worse, and Lily is afraid of storms."

"She's with Evie and Beth; she'll be okay. We're heading back in the morning, so there's no need to hike back a mile to the truck in this storm. Call her if you're worried," Cash advised, throwing two poker chips into the pile in front of him.

King didn't say anything, seeing Shade's concern for Lily. Instead, he crushed his cigar into the ashtray and got to his feet.

"What are you doing?" Shade paused putting on his jacket.

"Going with you." King put on his boots then his jacket.

"There's no need for you to leave."

"We're going back in a few hours anyway; might as well go now."

Shade didn't argue further as King reached to open the door after grabbing one of the flashlights.

"Wait a minute. Let me get my things; I'm going, too," Razer said, getting up from the table and gathering his things.

"Fuck, if you guys go, then I have to go. Winter will throw it up to me that you came running back to your women, and I'll never hear the end of it."

"You pussy-whipped bastards are ruining all the fun," Cash said, getting to his feet.

As they gathered their things, King didn't know if it was the wisest decision to leave the safety of the cabin during a raging thunderstorm, but Shade's tension-filled face had King anxious to leave.

Cash locked the door behind them as a loud burst of thunder sounded from directly above.

King had no trouble keeping up with most of the men as they traveled through the forest; however, Shade traveled at a fast pace that was hard for any of them to match. He was waiting for them when they finally reached their vehicles. As soon as King, Cash, Rider, and Viper closed the truck door, he peeled out of the parking lot, leaving the rest to the other truck.

"Fuck, what's the hurry, Shade?" Cash asked from the backseat.

"The girls aren't answering their phones."

Chapter Twenty-eight

Evie rolled over in her bed then sat up; she thought she had heard a noise. Thinking it was just the thunder, she was about to lay back down when she thought she heard a noise again. She looked at her bedside clock and saw the illuminated numbers were missing. Fuck, the power must have gone out.

Getting up, she was putting on her housecoat when she saw her door was opening.

"Beth, what are…?"

"Shh…" Her frantic whisper had Evie snapping her mouth closed as she ran to her friend in the dark. "There are people trying to break in the front and back doors."

"Let's go to Lily's room and call the police. We can barricade ourselves in until the police get here. You got your phone?"

"No, I left it downstairs." Beth clutched her stomach, moaning.

"Beth!"

"Evie, get your phone. I'll go to Lily's room." As Beth went back out the door, Evie ran to her bedside table, picking up her phone. However, when she ran out of her bedroom, there was a masked man in the hallway coming toward her. He raised the gun in his hand, pointing it at her, and out of reflex, Evie threw her cell phone at his head. Frantically, she ran into the room she had given Lily, barely managing to shut the door.

"Help me!" Evie screamed as she battled the intruder trying to open the door.

"Move," Lily said.

Evie had no choice, the door swung open and when it did, Lily brought the bedside lamp down on the intruder's head. Evie pushed him backward as he fell, knocking him back into the hallway. Lily and Evie then both slammed the door shut, locking it quickly.

"Help me slide the dresser in front of the door," Evie said, moving to the side of the dresser and beginning to push it toward the door. Lily quickly helped, sliding the heavy furniture until they finally managed to get it in front of the door.

"Evie!" Beth moaned.

She ran to Beth who was sitting on the floor by the bed, panting.

"My babies are coming."

"Relax, Beth."

"Don't tell me to relax! There are burglars outside the door, and my babies are coming early."

"Lily, where's your phone?"

"I'm looking. It was on the dresser." Evie saw Lily searching the floor for the phone while she examined Beth.

The sound of a gunshot striking the door drew screams from each of them.

"Lily, get down!"

Evie put her hands under Beth's arms, dragging her to the other side of the bed, pushing the mattress and box springs off the bed so it would place a barrier in front of Beth.

"Lily, get behind the mattress," Evie screamed at her when another gunshot came through the door.

"I have to find my phone. It's the only chance we have," Lily said, running her hands over the floor. "Please, God. Please, God, help us." Evie's heart broke at hearing Lily's praying as she searched.

She crawled back to Beth who was crying, trying to stifle her screams. Evie pulled up Beth's gown to exam her, seeing the crown of one of the babies' head.

"Beth, listen to me. The first baby is coming, which means we're going to have to do this alone. I've delivered a few babies, so I know what to do, okay? We can do this."

Beth whimpered, "Okay."

"I found it!"

"Thank, God," Evie muttered. "I need something to cut the cord with."

"I keep a small pen knife in my purse. It's on the nightstand," Lily answered. "I'm calling 911."

"Tell them to send an ambulance," Evie instructed her. The first baby was out now. She jerked the pillowcase off the pillow, carefully wrapping the baby in it as soon as she made sure the baby boy was breathing. She cut the cord using the penknife she found in Lily's purse.

She looked over her shoulder to see Lily crying.

"My phone isn't working. It must have broken when we moved the dresser," Lily whispered in a low voice, but Evie knew Beth heard above the crying infant.

The sound of the men hitting their shoulders against the door had both of them rising to see over the mattresses; the door was practically bulging inward under the intruders' attacks. However, Beth's scream drew Evie back to her.

"Dammit, can anything else go wrong!" Evie said then could have kicked herself. She didn't want to alarm Beth.

"What?" Lily dropped back down beside her.

"Hold the baby." Evie took the baby away from Beth, giving it to Lily.

"Evie?" Beth's faint whisper as she frantically tried to stem the flow of blood escaping her had Evie more terrified than she had been in her life.

Her training kicked in as she worked, making herself focus on saving Beth and her children, not the crashing of the door or the sounds of footsteps entering the room. She didn't take her eyes off Beth when she heard the steps stop beside Lily. Evie began crying, knowing the next sound she heard was going to be Lily being killed.

"Please, don't hurt the baby." Evie cried helplessly as she heard Lily pleading to the intruder. "Please."

As a gunshot rang through the room then three more, one after another, Evie didn't stop what she was doing.

"Lily!" Evie heard Shade's voice.

"Call an ambulance!" Evie screamed as the room filled with The Last Riders. "And get my medical bag out of my bedroom closet."

A minute later, the bag was next to her.

"The ambulance is on the way," King stated, moving away.

"Beth!" Razer tried to get to Beth, but there was not enough room. The room erupted with the men as they moved the bodies then the bed out of the way.

"Beth." Razer's voice broke as he managed to reach her hand.

Evie glanced up at him. She didn't have to say anything; the blood seeping everywhere said it all.

* * *

The large hospital waiting room was filled with silence. Evie sat next to King, holding his hand tightly. She was wearing a set of scrubs one of the nurses had gotten for her when she had stepped into the waiting room, covered in Beth's blood. The EMTs had delivered the second baby en route to the hospital.

"Do you need me to get you something?" King offered.

"No." Evie brushed her tears away. They hadn't even come out to tell them if the babies were doing okay.

"I've known some scary situations in my life, but when

I heard those gunshots and couldn't get to you and Lily…" Evie clung to his hand tighter, hearing King's hoarse voice. She had to reassure him she was fine.

Razer sat next to her as if turned to stone while Lily and Shade sat on the other side.

One by one, each of the members of The Last Riders entered the room. Evie looked up anxiously when the door opened to see Sex Piston and her crew come in, followed by a grim-faced Stud.

The door to the waiting room remained open. There was a line of bikers down both sides of the long hallway. Not only were there The Last Riders that couldn't fit in the room, but the members from the Blue Horsemen and the Destructors.

Evie's eyes watered. Beth's simple friendship with Sex Piston had created a bridge between the groups who should have been enemies. Sex Piston had been a true friend to Beth when Evie herself had failed.

The woman so filled with attitude, that drove everyone crazy and loved very few, knelt in front of Razer, placing her hand on his thigh. "When I met Beth, I thought there was no way she could be for real. No one could be that sweet or clueless. As I got to know her, I realized she was the most real person I have ever met."

"The last month of my pregnancy, I was scared, afraid of the delivery, the pain, of being a mom." Tears coursed down Sex Piston's cheeks. "She told me not to be afraid, that I had to have faith that everything would be all right. Razer, we're both going to listen to Beth and have faith that she and those precious babies are all going to be fine."

Razer's composure broke as he took Sex Piston into his arms, and Evie turned into King's chest as her own tears fell.

"Evie, listen to her. Beth is going to be okay," King murmured, trying to soothe her.

"I was a terrible friend to her," Evie cried. The guilt of years ago had never left her.

"You saved her life—our lives," Lily contradicted her. "Tonight, when those men came, you didn't leave her side. You delivered her son, and the doctor told us it was your skills as a Corpsman that kept her alive until the ambulance came. Beth considers you more than a friend— she loves you like a sister—and I do, too."

"Excuse me." The exhausted doctor standing in the doorway eyed the rough-looking crowd waiting for news.

Razer rose shakily to his feet.

"Your wife is in recovery. It will be at least an hour before you can see her." He motioned to the nurse. "Shelley will take you to the nursery. There are two boys waiting to meet their dad."

* * *

Beth's head turned on her pillow, her fingers closing on the hand holding hers.

"Razer," she said softly.

Razer lifted his head, rising up on his elbow next to her.

"I don't think you're supposed to be in the bed with me," she warned him weakly.

"Shade will knock on the door when someone is about to come into the room."

She turned her head into his shoulder, and his hand came down to rest on the top of her head.

"If our babies aren't okay, please don't tell me, Razer. I couldn't take it."

"Our sons are in the nursery, and they're fine. They want to wait before they bring them in, though. Your vitals are still weak, so as soon as they get higher, they'll bring them in."

"Boys?"

"Two sons. You did good, kitten." His voice choked on her nickname.

"We both did. Lily and Evie?"

"They're waiting to see you."

"I thought we were going to die. Lily didn't even ask

for her own life; she just asked them not to hurt the baby." Tears broke free. "And Evie kept trying to deliver the baby. She saved us, Razer."

"You had two angels with you. When we pulled in the driveway and saw the front door open and the lights out, we knew something was wrong. If Shade wasn't such a good shot… he killed those bastards before I could get in the front door."

Beth shuddered against him.

"Kitten, I've never been so scared in my life. When I saw you, I thought I was going to lose you."

"Razer, you're never going to lose me. Even if I died, I would always be with you."

"Don't talk like that again! You're not allowed to use the words 'I' and 'die' in the same sentence. You're not allowed to die before me, ever! You think you couldn't bear to lose our sons? Well, I couldn't lose you and stay sane. Kitten, I know what life is without you.

"If I died…" Shocked, Beth tried to stop his words, but his finger pressed against her lips, halting her words. "If I died," he continued, "you would be strong enough to carry on and raise our children. Eventually, you would make it through life until we could be together again. Me, on the other hand, I am an asshole. If I couldn't have you, then there wouldn't be anything of me left to give anyone."

"Baby," she kissed the finger pressed against her lips, "I'm not going anywhere. We're going to raise those two boys, and you're going to be stuck with me for a long time. I promise."

"I'm going to go see if the nurse will bring the babies in." Razer gently raised the bed to where she was almost sitting up.

"Yes, please."

"I almost forgot." Reaching into his pocket, he pulled something out then took her hand in his, sliding her wedding and engagement rings back on with the same look on his face that had been there on their wedding day. She felt his hesitation at leaving her, his eyes on the machines plugged into her.

"Go, Razer. I'll be right here waiting..."

King nodded to Shade, who gently clicked the door shut before Razer could catch them, then strolled down the hallway, relieved that his young cousin would be fine and she held nothing other than love in her heart for Evie.

Chapter Twenty-nine

Evie knocked on the hospital room's door, going in when Razer opened it.

She carried the heavy packages into the room with King carrying more behind her, coming to a stop by her friend's bed. Looking down at Beth's exhausted face as she held the two babies swaddled in blue blankets, she said a brief prayer of thanks before putting the bags on the chair beside the bed.

"I packed you a suitcase. I put a couple of gowns in it, your new housecoat, your make-up bag and your hair brush." She lifted up a blue book bag then set it back down. "I also bought you some magazines and crossword puzzles. I found your Kindle; it's in there, too. I also sent you an e-certificate to purchase books, so knock yourself out."

She turned, taking a little, baby-blue suitcase from King. "I brought the suitcase you had packed for the babies, too. I took out the pink ones you had packed and put in more boy clothes. I went through all your shower gifts and picked out what you needed before you got home and packed those, too."

She turned to King again, taking the flowers and

217

balloons from him before setting the flowers on the bedside table. Putting the teddy bear holding the balloons on her bed, she went to Beth's side.

"Can I hold one?" she asked.

Beth closed her mouth, lifting her cradled bundle toward Evie. "You can hold them both." Laughing, she handed King the other one.

King gently took the baby, lifting it to his chest. "He's beautiful."

"Thank you." Evie smiled at Razer's proud comment.

When King lowered the baby into her other arm, Evie looked down at the babies, ad-miring their tiny fingers.

"Evie." She looked up when Beth called her name. "There are no words to say how much I appreciate what you did. You saved my babies' lives. I owe you a debt I can never repay."

"Beth—"

"Let me finish, please. Razer told me what you said in the waiting room. I want you to know that, when I lashed out at you after Razer and I broke up, I was hurt and angry. I didn't understand the loyalty you felt to The Last Riders back then, but I do now. I want you to forgive yourself, because I did a long time ago. Okay?"

Evie nodded her head, too choked up to speak.

Sex Piston came in the door then, breaking the emotional moment. Killyama, Crazy Bitch, Fat Louise and T.A. each filed into the room next, their arms full of bags, balloons and stuffed animals.

Sex Piston bent over the bed, hugging Beth. "Don't fucking scare me like that again."

"I won't."

Sex Piston rose, eyeing the big teddy bear on the bed with the balloons. She turned, looking at the items sitting around. Putting her hands on her hips, she narrowed her eyes, looking at Evie who was holding both babies. "You gonna share?"

"You going to cuss when you're holding them?"

"I'm not going to make any promises," she said, taking the one sleeping.

"What are their names?" T.A. asked, taking the other one from Evie.

"We haven't decided yet." Razer sat down on the bed beside his wife.

Evie stood up, giving Beth and Razer a hug. "Let me know when you need a babysitter."

"I think it's going to be a while before I let them out of my sight again." Razer followed them out the door into the hallway, closing the door behind them.

"I thought Lily would be in the room with Beth?" Evie questioned.

"She was here earlier, but Shade made her go home to get some rest. She'll be back later. She and Shade will stay while I go home to get some sleep." Evie saw Rider and Train sitting in chairs in the waiting room. "Are they waiting to see Beth and the babies?"

"No, the brothers want to keep a guard on them until we can get them home."

"Why?" Concerned, Evie stopped walking; Razer's fierce expression told her something was wrong.

"Because Knox got an ID on those men who broke into your house; they were profes-sionals. Until we find out what they wanted, we're going to watch all three of you. We talked to King; he's going to stay with you, and we have both Beth and Lily covered."

Evie grabbed King's arm, feeling like she was going to faint.

"Evie!" King turned, catching her.

"I'm fine. I'm just tired after being awake almost forty-eight hours. I'm going home to bed. I'll see you tomorrow."

"Later." Razer didn't look like he believed her, but she had to talk to Shade. She could be wrong, but if she was right, then the only way to catch the person responsible was to let whoever was behind the attack believe the case was closed because the suspects were dead.

They drove back to King's house, and as soon as the door closed behind them, King turned her to face him. "It had nothing to do with me. I called Henry; everything is quiet in Queen City."

"This has nothing to do with you. We both know who is responsible."

"Brooke? Do you think she believes she can have Shade if she removes the obstacles in her way?"

"No, I don't think so. I believe it's more like, if she can't have him, then no one can." Evie took off her shoes. "I had hoped the baby would calm her down, make her a little more human. I guess I was wrong."

"Evie, we don't know anything for certain. This is all speculation. We don't know for sure."

Evie did know, remembering the gunman standing beside Lily. The gun had been pointed at her.

"I'll never forget Lily begging for that baby's life."

"Evie, it's over. Beth, the babies, Lily—you're all alive. Nothing else matters. Go on to my room and take a shower. I'll bring you a glass of wine."

"Fuck that, bring me a whiskey."

"All right. I'll be there in a minute."

Evie went to King's bedroom. She had showered earlier when she picked up Beth's shower presents, so another wasn't needed.

She was pulling off her jeans when she looked across the room. Grinning wickedly, she kicked her jeans away.

As King came into the bedroom, carrying their glasses, a flash of movement caught his eye. "I see you found my surprise." He set their glasses down on the nightstand.

"This one is better than mine," Evie said from the top of the pole.

"I was afraid you were going to break your neck on the one you had. Henry arranged for that one to be shipped for me."

"Who installed it?" Evie asked, flipping herself upside-down.

King unbuttoned his shirt, removing his clothes without taking his eyes off her body. He lay down naked on the bed, picking up his whiskey before he leaned back against the headboard, enjoying the show. "I don't understand why you constantly believe I can't do the same shit normal men do."

Evie stopped spinning to stare across the room at him. Even naked, he looked elegant and sophisticated. "How did the fishing trip go? Catch anything?"

"No. Only Cash and Shade did. My son-in-law is beginning to give me a complex," he complained, finishing his drink then setting his glass down.

Evie laughed, working her way down the pole.

"I didn't see your fishing pole when Cash dropped your stuff off at my place. Where's it at?"

"At the bottom of the lake," King admitted reluctantly.

Evie laughed, twirled around the bottom of the pole then turned her back to it, sliding down it into a full squat.

"Come here."

Evie sashayed across the room, crawling from the bottom of the bed to kneel beside him. "So, who installed the pole?"

"Train and Rider."

Evie reached out, trailing her fingers teasingly along the tip of his cock. "Did you enjoy the show?"

"Can't you tell?"

Evie bent over, sucking the tip of his cock into her mouth. His hand went to her hair, pulling it back from her face, holding it in one hand.

"Henry's mailing me a couple of other packages, too. I thought, since you would be do-ing a show for me, you might as well have a costume."

"Which one?" Evie's head raised a fraction of an inch.

"The red lace one for me, and the dominatrix for you."

When Evie's head lowered again, sucking him to the back of her throat, he groaned as her tongue curled around him, her fingers going for his balls. Her mouth then slid up his length again.

"Did you tell him to mail the flogger, too?"

"That, I might have forgotten." Evie started to rise up, but the hand in her hair prevented her. "I thought you might want to pick your own out online."

"That'll work." Her head went back down, her mouth closing over him again.

"Of course, I get to try it out first." That was a win-win situation as far as she was con-cerned.

When he was about to come, he used his hand in her hair to take her mouth off his nearly bursting cock. Leaning forward, he maneuvered her to straddle him, sinking every inch into her wet pussy. Taking a nipple in each hand to rub, he watched his cock disappear inside her.

"I think we should go out of town next weekend." King said, watching her nipples thrust out, begging to be sucked. He leaned forward, licking one.

Evie was about to come, sliding up and down his dick. Her fingers went to her clit as he fucked her. "Okay." She was barely paying attention the more her orgasm climbed.

"I've wanted to get my cock pierced. What do you think?" He grinned against her breast.

Evie came, her knees gripping King's hips as she ground out her orgasm until she lay weak and spent on his chest. "I think that's an excellent idea."

* * *

Evie answered the knock at her door. She had come downstairs to get more boxes. King wanted her to move in with him, and as much as she loved her new house, she wanted to live with him more.

The bedroom was a constant reminder of the men that had been killed upstairs. The tragedy that had almost happened had her anxious to finish getting her things packed to avoid going up there anymore.

She wasn't surprised to see Knox on the other side of

the door. He had called earlier to ask if he could stop by.

"Hey, Evie."

"Knox." She closed the door behind him. "Want a cup of coffee?"

"Sounds good."

They went in to the kitchen where Evie poured them both a cup.

Knox leaned against the counter drinking his.

"What's the news you said you needed to tell me?"

"The IDs came back on the men. They were from Georgia."

Evie leaned shakily against the counter. Evie knew her sister hated her, but to do so to the extent of actually having someone kill her was frightening. There was no doubt in her mind Brooke was responsible for the break-in.

"I asked the police to check into a possible connection with Brooke and the men. They informed me that there wasn't enough evidence to pursue an investigation.

"My father's family has a lot of influence."

"So I've gathered. I asked a couple of my buddies stationed there if they would check into it for me, though. We both know she's covered her tracks, and as all the intruders are dead, it's not like we can get them to turn on her. We're pretty much at a standstill until something turns up. I'm sorry, Evie."

"It's what I expected." Evie set her cup down on the counter next to his. "I can't believe she hates me so much as to actually try to kill me."

"The thing is, from how you described the break in, I don't believe you were the main target."

Evie felt the color drain from her face. The fact she was related to someone so evil turned her stomach.

Knox took her into his arms, holding her close. "It will be all right. Shade is watching out for Lily, and King has your back. She's not stupid enough to try something again. She knows we're on to her."

"So she gets away again scot-free?"

"I'm afraid so."

Evie gave a bitter laugh. "She was responsible for my rape, and indirectly, Levi's and Sunshine's deaths, now this. They would still be alive if not for me." The guilt she had har-bored inside for years showed in her haunted eyes. She had punished herself in every possible way for living while they had died.

"Evie, you weren't responsible for either of their deaths. Levi was killed in a fight, and Sunshine was killed by a bomb. Levi could have left the bar earlier, and Sunshine knew the dangers when she joined the service."

"But… If I hadn't gotten raped, then neither of them would have been there."

"You. Were. Not. Responsible for your rape! Those bastards were. I've told you this over and over. Evie, believe me; after Sunshine died, I wanted someone to blame, to help me deal with the pain, so believe me when I say it wasn't your fault. Are you finally going to believe me?"

Evie nodded her head against his chest.

"You're happy now?"

"Yeah. Diamond and I are meant to be together. No one else could put up with her nuttiness. She practically turned our spare bedroom into a bomb shelter. You?"

Evie laughed, raising her head. "Yes, but King couldn't fix a leak if his life depended on it."

"I can't, either. Rider was always the handyman."

"I don't know about that," Evie joked, pulling away to refill their cups.

As she turned, she heard King coming down the steps. Reaching into the cabinet, she pulled out another cup.

"Knox," King greeted him when he entered the room.

"King." The men looked at each other guardedly.

Evie poured King his coffee as Knox repeated what he had told her about the break in.

Evie handed King his cup, meeting his worried eyes.

"There's nothing else we can do?"

"No."

"Is it safe for Lily to be at the church store?"

"I believe so. Brooke is smart; she's not going to do anything that will cast suspicions on her," Knox said grimly, setting down his cup. "I better be getting back to the office. Take care, Evie."

"I will." Evie walked him back to the door. When she returned to the kitchen, King was sitting at the table, looking thoughtful.

"You don't seem upset." he said.

"It was what I expected." Evie sat down at the table. "I'm praying Brooke will be frightened she almost got caught."

"If not?"

"She fucked up this time, whether she realizes it or not. I have every confidence that Shade will deal with Brooke."

"The sooner the better."

Evie gave a sarcastic laugh. "She has no idea of who she's dealing with, King."

He started laughing.

"What's so funny?"

"I never thought I would see the day that I was actually glad Shade's a cold-hearted bastard."

Epilogue

As King flipped the sizzling burger, feeling like it was him on fire under the late summer sun, Shade walked up to him with a beer in his hand, giving it to him.

"Thanks." King took a long drink of the cold beer.

"Want me to take over for a while?" Shade offered.

"Don't even think about it. Evie doesn't think I can do anything macho. This is me about to prove her wrong."

"Grilling is macho?" Shade's eyes took in his sweaty t-shirt.

"Isn't it?" King asked, wiping the perspiration from his brow with a paper towel.

"You're not going to feel very manly when you suffer a heat stroke."

"Just keep the beers coming; the burgers are almost ready."

The crowd had gathered in the backyard of the clubhouse for Beth and Razer's sons' baptisms. Many were waiting to be fed, already making their plates from the buffet the women had put together.

Thank Christ, he was able to finish cooking the last of the burgers. Then he sought the shade of one of the trees where tables had been set out.

Evie waved at him from across the yard, holding one of Beth's sons while the other baby was in his father's arms. He couldn't tell which one Evie was holding from where he was sitting, but he was almost certain it was Noah. Evie would never admit it, but she had grown attached to the baby she had delivered.

Chance was smaller, but he was a fighter. He had been born blue. Beth had said her son was given another chance at life. King looked down at the wedding ring on his finger; the little boy wasn't the only one who had been given a second chance.

He and Evie, with Lily and Shade, had a quiet ceremony in his backyard. Lucky performed the ceremony, and it was the most beautiful moment of his life.

Coming out of his reverie, he saw Lily coming out of her house, carrying a large book. When she saw him sitting under the tree, she walked over to the table.

"What are you doing sitting over here by yourself?"

"Taking a breather," King admitted to his daughter.

Lily laughed, sitting at the table next to him and setting the book down in front of him. "I made this for you."

"For me?" Surprised, King reached out, opening the scrapbook to find pictures of Lily at the age he had left her with Beth's parents.

"I was eight here."

"I know." King turned the page, looking at several more pictures of Lily. In one, she was in church, another she was sitting beside Beth. There was even one of her playing with a doll.

King reached out a trembling hand, turning another page. On this one, she appeared to be slightly older; getting on the school bus, playing on the school playground, in a mermaid costume during a Halloween party.

"I was nine here," Lily said, placing her hand over his. She turned the pages slowly, showing him her life one page at a time. The shadows and pain in her eyes were always there until she came to the next to the last page.

On that page, she had her wedding pictures, and nothing was in her eyes other than happiness.

"Lily…"

"I didn't give you this book to show you what you've missed but to share with you what a wonderful life you gave me. Thank you."

King could only nod. If he cried, all The Last Riders would see, as well as Evie. Macho men didn't cry.

"There's one more picture I want you to see." Lily turned to the final page. On it was a picture of a sonogram. "I wanted you to be the first to know. Shade and I are going to have a baby. Dad, you're going to be a grandfather."

King looked down at the picture, crying. He was the first out of all the people she loved she gifted with the news of her child. The tiny child in that picture was his grandchild.

"You haven't even told Shade?" His voice was thick with emotion.

"Not yet."

As both of them watched Shade walking toward them, King closed the scrapbook.

"Are you ready to eat?" Shade asked Lily. King brushed the tears away from his cheeks.

"No, would you mind going to the car? I left a pack of diapers on the backseat, I thought we could…" Lily began mischievously.

"No. I am not making another diaper anything. I don't care who it's for." Shade broke off his rant, taking a good look at King's face. "Is Evie…?"

"No," King said, unable to hold back his smile any longer.

Shade looked back and forth between them. His face broke into a smile as he lifted Lily from her seat, twirling her around in his arms.

"What's going on?" Evie asked as she came to stand next to him. "Have you been crying?"

"Yes," King admitted.

"Why?"

"Lily called me Dad."

Also by Jamie Begley

The Last Riders Series:

Razer's Ride

Viper's Run

Knox's Stand

Shade's Fall

The VIP Room Series:

Teased

Tainted

King

Biker Bitches Series:

Sex Piston

The Dark Souls Series:

Soul Of A Man

Soul Of A Woman

About The Author

"I was born in a small town in Kentucky. My family began poor, but worked their way to owning a restaurant. My mother was one of the best cooks I have ever known, and she instilled in all her children the value of hard work, and education.

Taking after my mother, I've always love to cook, and became pretty good if I do say so myself. I love to experiment and my unfortunate family has suffered through many. They now have learned to steer clear of those dishes. I absolutely love the holidays and my family puts up with my zany decorations.

For now, my days are spent writing, writing, and writing. I have two children who both graduated this year from college. My daughter does my book covers, and my son just tries not to blush when someone asks him about my books.

Currently I am writing four series of books- The Last Riders, The Dark Souls, The VIP Room, and Biker Bitches series.

All my books are written for one purpose- the enjoyment others find in them, and the expectations of my fans that inspire me to give it my best. In the near future I hope to take a weekend break and visit Vegas that will hopefully be this summer. Right now I am typing away on my next story and looking forward to traveling this summer!"

Jamie loves receiving emails from her fans,
JamieBegley@ymail.com

Find Jamie here,
https://www.facebook.com/AuthorJamieBegley

Get the latest scoop at Jamie's official website,
JamieBegley.net

Printed in Great
Britain
by Amazon